DOWN THE DRAIN

DRAIN

BY

CHAUNCEY

HAWORTH

Chapters

Preface

There have been a few pieces of media that I have taken in over the years that have ruined my life. Maybe that's not fair? Maybe the problem lies with me? Maybe I have taken these perfectly innocent pieces of media, these happy little dreams of other storytellers, and distorted them into my own personal demons?

I'm sure that sounds melodramatic and makes little sense, so I'll do my best to explain.

I have always been drawn more to worlds than specific stories. I am the consumer that cinematic universes were marketed for, I guess.

When I was in 4th grade I read The Lord of the Rings Trilogy. My, what a smart kid I was right..? not really. I had seen the movie (the Ralph Bakshi animated one) and loved it so much that I ramrodded my way through the book. I can't remember, but I assume that I loved it, but didn't understand it much, because I read it every two years after that until I was about 16. I that point I must have had a good enough understanding of it finally to not have read it again... except once in my twentes...

To compound the overwhelming influence of that epic, through elementary school my favorite TV show was Robotech, 83 episodes of high-flying sweet transforming robot alien action… loosely muddled around a serious romantic soap opera for boys. Every day I would fight with my brother for the TV. He wanted to watch Days of Our Lives.

I loved the main 80s toys for boys like He-Man, Transformers, G.I. Joe, and the likes.

As I got older I moved on to horror and science fiction movies and their infinite sequels, spinoffs, ripoffs, and "Homages".

I could go on but I think I have rambled until I have reached the point. The point is I have been tainted by world-building. My love of epic and ongoing mythologies led me to believe that everything I ever created wasn't big enough, wasn't long enough, wasn't grand enough.

Then, babies, life, jobs, a wife, all the stuff that came in between. An important story to me, but probably not to you.

Over the years I attempted to create so many times and every time it wasn't enough and it would be scrapped. A story outline here, half a story there, a band with some songs here, a demo album there, half a comic here, flushed out characters there, and on and on.

Finally, after years of failure and quitting I came to the realization. The realization that if I put them all together into one world, then my failures would become what I felt I couldn't do.

So that's what you are going to start reading. A collection of decades of repeated failure… lucky you.

Angelica's Thereafter

MOTEL

Angelica's Thereafter

Angelica stepped out of the room she had gotten for the night at The Gentleman Grey Motel, into the morning sun, proceeded to the warmed asphalt of the motor lodge's expansive parking lot, and eyed for the location of her "Brown-Beater". She was buzzing with excitement. It had been a wild few days. Her first byline writing gig, the revival-meeting-style concert of the band Ivan Rocket and the Blackness Between the Stars followed by two days held up in a shitty roach motel writing and drinking coffee, and now this. Today is the day. Today she is no longer Miss Whateley, spoiled offspring of a B-list father, she is Angelica Whateley, Music Journalist Extraordinaire. Today her story was published.

The show in question was a trip, not only in means of driving, but a bit of a mindfuck as well, but one doesn't pursue being a music writer unless one is fan enough to have been to some wild shows on some wild substances, but this one, this one was a trip beyond. Making it all the more unbelievable was that when taken in bits, it all felt so normal.

She had arrived a little late but it ended up being just in time, time enough to meet Nicolas, the band's manager, have a drink, and walk to the back to interview the man himself, Ivan Rocket.

Ivan was an odd combination of an old soul and a newborn, touting deep thoughts mixed in with pot jokes and giggles, but he did seem to know something about her. They had never met and still, he seemed to know her. It all seemed very intuitive, very natural, like meeting a friend.

Then the show. It was in some sort of church revival tent and was delivered like a healing session to an oddly diverse collection of types of people, middle-America football guys, puritan spinsters, make-up wearing punks and goths, pink-lipped blue-eyeshadowed Bettys, and a whole lot more. During the show, she wasn't sure if it was the drink or the smoke, she started to see things. She saw black shadows as she was compelled to dance, to move, but the lights were wild, and she was drinking and smoking a bit. Eventually, it was more than she could stand and she left the tent. As she left she felt free like a heavy weight had been lifted from her. Was she healed by Ivan's music or was she high on her first paying show gig? She may never know, she didn't really care. All she knew now was that from there, the story of the night just came to her, and from there to her fingers, and then effortlessly spilled out onto the page.

With the article completed, submitted, and today being published, she practically skipped down to the lobby. She arrived at the continental breakfast station. If "continental" really meant "coming from, or characteristic of, mainland Europe", Europe must have some gross ass breakfast. It wasn't much more than a vinyl kitchen counter built into a room that looked like an office meeting room. On the counter was a dryer rack looking stand of cheap wood with plastic tubes of cereal, a stand of donuts, a stand of muffins, a few other prewrapped things, and what she wanted, coffee. She Grabbed a muddy cup of coffee and stepped to the news rack. She looked at the papers. The liberal news one, the conservative news one, the money one, and then hers, The Arkham Music Review. She picked it up and to her astonishment the cover said. "Rock n' Roll's New Revival: Ivan Rocket and the Blackness Between the Stars" and beneath it in infinitely small, italic font, "by Angelica Whateley".

"I got the cover," she whispered to herself with a self-indulgent fist pump and hovered with delight to an empty

7

table by the window.

It wasn't the most creative title, but it wasn't pandering to the lowest common denominator part of a journalist's job? In the world of music journalism, this was not what one would call a "big step" or "big money". Arkham and its surrounding areas had a bit of a music boom about twenty-or-so years ago, but not much since, but to Angelica, it was a start, a start down the pathway to independence.

Angelica was a weird conundrum. She wanted to be independent so she could be like normal twenty-somethings and had no idea that normal-twentysomethings had no interest in being independent. The family she was born into, The Whateleys were incredibly rich and known historically as learned men and adventurers, but, just to kick her weird upbringing into high gear, her father took that wealth and reputation to a new level. He took it to the television.

Her father's show was Investigation: Mystery with Professor Johnathan Whateley, a mouth full of a title for a show that was treated as tabloid more than anything else. But, for some reason, probably due to Professor Whateley's odd personality, it had surpassed cult status and was comfortably nudged into pop status, which meant Angelica's life was on display too. Add to that, her father was almost like some kind of cult leader, having other odd people living at the house like monks and healers. His personal bodyguard even claimed to be a demon that had been blessed. She shared a birthday with an old man that lived with them named Buster, his delivery driver that he referred to as his "logistics guy". Sure, that doesn't seem weird except that when they had a shared birthday dinner when she was twelve, her strawberry cake said 12, while his cake, that was really more of a side for black coffee in the form of a cinnamon swirl bundt cake said 182.

On top of that everyone knew she lived in the weird house. She wasn't classy enough for the rich kids and was too rich for the poor kids. Her life was such an open wound to be poked that nobody ever even really harassed her when her father ended up marrying a man.

Looking down at the luxurious continental donut pile and sugar smack plastic cereal tubes she thought that if this is what independent breakfast looks like, I'll gladly go back to the madhouse of my youth.

She started to read but was stopped by the jingle and buzz of her phone. She answered.

"You got the cover," the gruff, slightly irritated voice said over the phone. The voice was August Tierney, Owner-Editor of The Arkham Music Review and Angelica's boss.

"I got the cover," Angelica repeated back to him with unmasked satisfaction.

"You did good, Girlie," his twanged voice cut through the cheap burner phone speaker. "Ready for another?"

"Yes I am, Mr. Tierney," Angelica responded with obvious exaggeration.

It was funny how serious Mr. Tierney took all this. She was getting paid, but not that much, but then again, she was having fun taking it seriously too. Maybe Mr. Tierney found the secret to life? To enjoy taking all the things you do seriously? If he was enjoying it, his droopy jowls weren't giving it away.

"Good. Booky's sending you the job now," he said. "Keep moving this fast and writing at this quality and you'll have all the work you want, Girlie. Call me after the show."

"Thank you," she acknowledged, hearing the hang-up-click halfway through her statement, then a new alert dinged from the phone's speakers.

She opened the email from Booky, Mr. Tierney's assistant. The email was basic and to the point, as they always were. It read:

Show in Bolton. Prep Goth Band. Down the Drain. Friday Night.

She tapped the screen off and headed to the Brown-Beater with her coffee and newspaper in hand.

Angelica,
Down the Drain

Angelica, Down the Drain

~1~

Angelica stepped from the Brown-Beater and gently shut the car door behind her. On her drive to Bolton, she'd decided that her new article byline may not have paid her enough to get a new car, but it did give her a new outlook. Her poor degraded, ramshackle of a ride would henceforth be known as Lucille. There are many that might argue that her car was a boy-car, due to its wrinkly seats and weathered exterior. However, she thought there may be a time in her life that she would have a wrinkly seat and a weathered exterior and didn't feel that would make her want to be mistaken as a boy-person… and she'd be damned if anybody was going to gender shame Lucille.

It was noonish and the sun was shining on her face giving her a warm glow. It'd been a long time since she enjoyed seeing daylight. The life of concerts and writing about them, the life that she was pursuing at that moment, didn't lend itself to vitamin D, she'd forgotten how much she missed it. She patted Lucille on the hood and then walked across the parking lot towards a large metal warehouse.

The warehouse was a huge, undecorated, utilitarian metal box, easily the size of a grocery store.

She heard a whistle and looked to her left to see a face poking around the far corner of the building and waving her over. From Angelica's distance, the person seemed extra small and quite possibly wearing mouse ears? "Oh great, a kid's show. Nothing worse than turning up to a show and finding out it's at a 21 and under club… no drinks… or at best sneaky parking lot drinks with some 18-year-old 'promoter' that thinks he stands a chance of getting lucky."

As she got closer she realized that this pocket-sized-person was actually a fully grown woman. She was about 5'2 at best and slight, but shapely. What Angelica thought to be mouse ears were, in fact, two puffballs of dyed light blue hair on the sides, "a la Princess Leia if she had chosen Death Star shapes instead of, what were they, bear claws?"

"Angelica!" the girl called out with a smile and got on her tippy toes in order to give Angelica a full around the neck hug. Angelica felt doubly uncomfortable, her arms hanging at her sides, hugged by a stranger, and noticing this micro-humans ample chest against her stomach and makeup face against her own chest.

The girl stepped back, but somehow managed to still be holding Angelica's hands, looking up, she said, "I'm Biscuit".

"That makes sense," Angelica quickly and uncomfortably quipped.

"I know, not the coolest nickname. You can blame my Grampa," Biscuit responded.

"Are you a member of the band?" Angelica inquired, becoming more and more aware of Biscuit's unbreakable death-grip on her hands, "…and can I have my hands back?"

"Oh totally," Biscuit answered sheepishly, unleashing her steel-like clamps, "Sorry, I'm a lover. Yeah, I'm in the band. Follow me."

Biscuit continued talking about nothing and everything as Angelica followed her into the warehouse. Inside was an expansive open space with concrete flooring and a large stage at the far end, and in the middle of the room, a group of young people talking.

As Angelica and Biscuit walked up to the group it thinned out a bit, people leaving to go to their sound and set-up jobs leaving only the band, Down the Drain.

Biscuit introduced Angelica to the group then introduced the band to Angelica. "The tall one is Two-Bit, he plays guitar and sings. The medium one is Carter, he also plays guitar, and these two ladies," Biscuit pointed to two almost identical Hispanic girls, "are Tiffany Tiffany and Debbie Debbie, known together as the Rock Pops." Angelica looked at the two and raised an awkward closed off, accidental flathanded vulcan greeting. They seemed welcoming enough as the slightly taller one winked and the other pointed with finger guns.

"What an odd bunch," Angelica thought to herself, taking in the amalgamated group. "Are these rich kids playing goth or goth kids playing Kanye meets Valley Girl?"

Biscuit had her hair in near-perfect blue puffs, light skin, 80's pink lip gloss, blue eyeshadow, and a leather corset with skirt, fishnets, and boots. The boots even had heels, making this tiny girl even tinier than initially guessed.

Two-Bit , the one that Biscuit had introduced as the singer/ guitar guy, was tall, well over six feet, with a blonde feathered pomp, a polo-style pink Izod shirt, form-fitting pleated slacks oddly matched with black eyeliner and lipstick and dress shoes.

Carter, the other guitar, matched Two-Bits motif quite well with matching makeup paired with blue boat shoes, no socks, white slacks, an inverted color Joy Division T-shirt, and a mint green sweater tied around his shoulders.

Finally, Tiffany Tiffany and Debbie Debbie had matching

suits on, schoolgirl uniforms with dark plaid skirts, white shirts with little ascots, and ratted black hair above black eyeliner, black lipstick, and black blush.

Angelica had decided she should have gotten her hands on a recording of the band, or at least had Booky send her something. She couldn't decide if they were death yacht rock or yacht death rock, or if there was even a difference between the two.

Angelica made the appropriate handshakes and nods, then asked, "How long until the show?"

"About three hours," Carter responded, meticulously adjusting his flopped over sweater arms so they hung evenly.

"Great!" Angelica exclaimed, "Did you want to do the interview now?"

The group seemed to chuckle in unison. "No," Carter returned, "We'll have to do it after the show, we'll feel more ourselves."

Seeing Angelica's confusion as to what to do in the meantime, Biscuit chimed in, "But. There's a great little bar and restaurant down the street you can have drinky-poos at, and get some dinner while we finish setting up. Everything is covered for you there, you just need to say your name at the door."

~2~

Angelica Walked into The Wave and Meadow, the "Great little bar and restaurant down the street" suggested by Down the Drain band member Biscuit, and marveled at what they thought to be a little place. The "little place", was in fact, a full surf n' turf steakhouse connected to an emerald eighteen-hole golf course called Bolton Downe Greens.

Angelica stepped to the maître d' and asked for a quiet table outside.

He looked down his romanesque nose with a glare, appearing to eyeball her thrift store sweater and Converse combo. "Your name?" he asked.

"Angelica… Whateley," her answer sounding like another question.

He looked down for a sec at a spiral book on his podium, looked up and said with a smile, "Ah, yes, Ms. Whateley, please follow me."

Angelica followed her svelte porter through the opulent dining room and marveled at the ornate wood carvings and argent silverware. He led her to a back patio with open fireplaces and running water and offered her a table away from the others. She sat down and thanked him. Reaching down to her bag she realized that the running water was coming from a koi pond right next to her table. She pulled her laptop out and thought to herself, "Maybe I should take money from Dad and Charles", then started to write about the first part of her experience with Down the Drain.

~3~

If there is one thing that you can rely on in life, it's that the time a concert says it's going to start is not when the concert is going to start. Knowing this, Angelica arrived thirty minutes after the show was scheduled to start to find Tiffany Tiffany and Debbie Debbie as they smoked their last pre-show cigarette behind the warehouse.

"Hey there, Angelica, go 'round front, we're about to start. They have your name at the door," the shorter of the two yelled to her.

Angelica walked in the front doors with just a nod from the doorman. The inside was packed, full of rich twenty-somethings that all looked like they'd passed out at a Skull and Bones frat house party and ended up getting drunken makeup drawn all over them.

There were half-naked girls and boys swinging from pulleys amid the fog machine mist and pseudo-water laser lighting shooting across the floor. Angelica couldn't tell if when she struck up a conversation with a fan if it would be about cutting one's self or stock options. These were the alpha preppies, the literal rich kids on LSD.

Before she could take in another moment of the bombastic emo fuckfest, the lights dropped to complete blackness. For a single second, she saw nothing and just heard hoots and hollers echo across the umbra.

Then, Down the Drain Started.

It was a thunder of guitars and flashing lights, a total assault on the senses, the music like Rammstein and Skrillex made a baby, beat it to near death and left it on the side of the road to grow up eating roadkill and turning tricks... Angelica didn't really like it, but in the interest of journalist excellence, she set her cynicism aside and redefined. "Okay, it's a Thrill Kill Kult or Bauhaus rehash that may have lost some sight of the message or the artistry," she thought. "That's not so bad, right?"

In front of her was a mound of bodies dancing, or fighting, or possibly fucking; a mound of bodies fuck-fighting? She could make out limbs and the occasional mohawk from the guy or girl who didn't get the yuppie-death-cult newsletter.

Beyond the horde of angry horndogs, was the stage and the band. The crowd was doing all the work, the band just stood there. Biscuit smiling with a cigarette hanging out of her mouth and both hands on the keyboard next to Two-Bit strumming away and screaming into a microphone. On the left Tiffany Tiffany and Debbie Debbie, both leaned back playing, staring up at the ceiling with indifference. On the right was Carter playing guitar. Angelica didn't particularly like the band's style, definitely didn't like their music, and didn't like having to wait until after the show to interview them, but she did think that Carter looked pretty good up there. "Fuck it," she thought and grabbed the closest drink she could find and walked toward the mob of fans to join the copulative melee. She had enough to write about, even if she woke up in a haze.

Biscuit,
Down the Drain

Biscuit, Down the Drain

~1~

After the show, Angelica found herself very drunk, very high, and having possibly done some cocaine, grabbed by Biscuit and Carter, and whisked away uncomfortably with the three of them stuffed in a two-seater headed out to the local lake to continue the party. That's how she found herself crammed in the passenger seat of an MR2 with Biscuit on her lap, beat-heavy music blaring, windows down while whizzing along the old highway at dizzying speeds.

Through the open window and a crook in Biscuit's crunched-up arm, Angelica could see trees wiping by in the darkness. Tall, aphotic timber capped with fir tree silhouettes. Every mile or so a single street light on the highway flashed a yellow tint onto the browns and greens of the forest, then quickly slapping back to the black and navy shadows.

The windows automatically went up and she felt the shuffling of bodies around her until, in her small window of view, Biscuit slowly lowered down a teensy-tiny spoon with cocaine in it. She slowly moved her head toward the snuff-spoon and gently plotted the intricate docking procedure. Can't exhale, can't move too quickly. She made contact, contracted her face to bend her nose to one side so as to close up one nostril as best she could, and gave a snuff. Up went the coke immediately helping her body to expel some of the effects of the booze.

Then she remembered. They said they were going out to Lake Hali, which they referred to as Nightmare Lake. The band had said they were, "Going to get fucked up and swim by the drain at Nightmare Lake", to which Angelica responded with, "Shit! I didn't bring a suit!", to which they responded with laughter. This, of course, Angelica did not like the sound of. She wasn't a hundred percent ashamed of her body, but that didn't mean she was a hundred percent not ashamed of it either.

But then, there was the story to entice her.

Carter had told her the story of the band's name, Down the Drain back at the warehouse after the show. They were sitting in a corner on a couch as some post-party fire dancers spit kerosene plums of flame into the air. She had asked, "why does your band have such a stupid name" in a partially flirty, partially insulting, and mostly drunken way. Then he leaned in close and told her.

~ 2 ~

Carter half-whispered in her ear and half yelled over the pumping music. "Back in the '70s or some shit, this lake was a total hot spot for well-to-do families vacationing in the summer. I mean, it was hoppin'. Boats, BBQs, bands, ya know, the whole shebang. There was this girl named Sara, I guess everyone called her Simple on account she was an A student that said 'simple' when asked a math problem when she was a kid. I guess the name stuck, cuz she's about 17 'er something at the time of the story."

Angelica enjoyed his hot liquor breath in her ear as he told the story. "She was traveling up with her newly divorced mom and her little 6-year-old brother. They are trying to get away due to the divorce and all the problems that came with it, one of which being that the boy had to sleep with all the lights on now and would scream in the dark. Weird shit right?" Carter asked Angelica with a look of excitement on his face as she was trying to look coy with a straw while listening and hoping that she didn't come across looking like a slut.

It must have been working because he seamlessly continued with a smile on his face. "So they are out there doing what people did, swimming and drinking PBR or whatever. So now the drain, the lake is manmade, you can't tell too much by the look of it, but it is, there's even a town and a bunch of trees down there that you can see if you go diving... and every dam has a spillway for emergency overflow… at least I think they all do. Anyway, normally they have tubes or ramps or other stuff, but some lakes have a drain. It's surreal. It's an actual fucking drain. Some of the locals call it the Gloryhole, but that shit's nasty so the locals try to call it the drain, cuz who wants to be from the town with the Gloryhole right?" he asked with a totally serious look on his face while pulling away for a second to sip his drink.

"It's a huge concrete hole at the water level about 40 feet across and about forty or fifty yards out, a literal drain I shit you not. Ever since the 20s, when the lake was opened, it was like a right of passage to swim out there and tap the rim and swim back, everyone knew it and everyone did it or wanted to." Angelica's Richy Rich view of the small town was getting some redneck vibes. I guess that they're nouveau riche

Carter continued, "The basics of the story are that the mom, being newly divorced, was drinking and flirting with lifeguards or whatever moms like to flirt with and Simple was off in the bushes getting to third base for the first time with some churchy kid named Chilly or something. We know it was third base because Chilly grew up to be some weird fucker that liked to tell the story. The little brother, wanting to be the new man of the house swam out to the drain… and fuckin' fell in."

At this point Angelica no longer felt flirty or sexy or confused by the money slash hick town confusion, she was intrigued. Carter went on, "Apparently, the mom and Simple were beside themselves freaking out, in the end, neither could get over his death, especially the fact that he fell in a long dark hole being so scared of the dark." There was a long pause, then, "In the end, the kid's body was never found due to the amount of muck and mud at the bottom, the mom killed herself, and Simple disappeared and was never seen again… or so the story goes.

Staring out the window at the city of trees speeding by she asked herself, "How was I going to turn down that story? If nothing else, I can brag to Charles about it."

~3~

In the parking lot of Nightmare Lake's marina area, the three of them came piling out of the microscopic MR2 like a clown car. Next to the car were two 80's-dated, but extremely fancy cars and a group of a few silhouettes walking down to the beach beckoning the trio to follow.

They went running after them, through the darkness, laughing. Angelica was relieved as she felt her feet start landing on sands and welcomed by the small campfire in front of her that illuminated part of the shore.

Including Angelica, there were seven of them. The Down the Drain band members, Carter, Two-Bit, Biscuit, Tiffany Tiffany, and Debbie Debbie, and the seventh was the soundman from the show she had met in the throng named Brad. Some of them were undressed and some were in a state of getting undressed. Tiffany Tiffany and Debbie Debbie were fully clothed and obviously angry.

"Turn it off, fuckhead," one of the Rock Pop twins said to Chad.

Biscuit leaned over to Angelica while shimmying out of her pants and panties at the same time and said, "It's a song by their old band when they were a duo. Chad loves it, but they kinda hate Chad."

Angelica listened. It was a beat and some electronics and some L'Trimm, *Cars that Go Boom* style rapping over it. Something about wanting to go to school and get a job.

"Fine, fine," the naked Brad conceded and tapped his phone, and the speaker on the blanket switched to the Down the Drain song, Sweet Light.

Angelica knew it was now or never. She had three options. One, not get undressed and get teased, sit on the sand with loud music, sobering up and bored. Two, stand dumbfounded by fear of the nakedness until they all made fun of her and she gave in, leaving her to undress while they watched and waited. She chose the third option, to get undressed while they did so as to blend into the crowd by the dimness of the campfire.

"Thanks, fucker," Tiffany Tiffany and Debbie Debbie said in practical unison and started to get undressed. They both had amazing bodies, perfectly fit and athletically shapely. Angelica's insides startled just a little bit when she noticed one significant difference between the two, one of them had a penis. She'd lived in cities and around diversion long enough to know to avert her gaze as naturally as possible and continue as life was before, but there is always that twinge of guilt for the moment of shock.

"I don't see why you always have to do that, Brad." The taller one bitched.

"Cuz I fucking love it, you know that ladies," he replied and chugged his beer and tossed the can into an open Trader Joe's bag.

"You're a dickhead," one of the two told him, then turned to Biscuit. "Are we doing this or what, Chicken n' Biscuits?"

"Fine," Biscuit said and asked Angelica, "Were gonna tap the drain, wanna come?"

"That's a hard pass," Angelica protested. "Cocaine, bourgeois death cult industrial metal, and showing my goods to a group of strangers is about as adventurous as I'm getting today, but I'll happily watch you do it."

"Now who's the Chicken n' Biscuits?" Biscuit asked the Pop Rock girls.

"You. You're still the chicken. This is Ange's first time out here, but you've been talking about this shit for weeks… if not years." She responded, then yelled, "Come on!" and ran out into the shallow water, her light brown body shining in the blend of dark water, sky, and mountains. Biscuit took off after her, tripping slightly as she hit the water, then diving forward into a swim to catch up.

"Deb Deb is a nut job, one reason why I love her," Brad said, watching as the duo disappeared into the murk.

"Shut up, creep," the other girl said to him. Angelica thought, "Okay, this one is Tiffany Tiffany making the other Debbie Debbie." Angelica quickly looked down, saw no penis, and made a mental note of which was which.

Carter handed Angelica a beer and asked her if she wanted to wade. She obliged as they both walked out, knee-deep into the tepid water, and talked.

25

~4~

"Wait up!" Biscuit yelled to Debbie Debbie, then realized that Debbie Debbie had one hand on the edge of the large concrete rim. With a final kick, Biscuit glided up next to her and grabbed the rim as well.

Debbie Debbie looked at her, smiled, and softly said, "Now the new girl is Chicken n' Biscuits."

The girls started laughing.

"Ok, let's head back and get some booze and tunes in our system before I lose my shit," Debbie said.

"One sec," Biscuit asked as she swung her leg over the side of the drain.

"What the fuck are you doing?" Debbie yelled.

"I'm gonna dive off it," she responded and before Debbie could stop her, Biscuit's knees were knocking as she tried to stand upright on the edge of the drain. Upon reaching a full arms up body extension, Biscuit hooted a howl of triumph, slipped, and fell backward into the drain as her victory call was swallowed up.

"Oh, Shit! Biscuit!" Debbie yelled, scrambling her arms over the rim and looking in. All she heard was her own echo. "Biscuit?" she pleaded softly into the black hole. "Can you hear me?" It was silent as she stared on in shock.

The moment was broken by a slight snap, like a twig, and then a subtle scratch like stones settling in a pile. As Debbie peered into the shades of black in the opening she saw movement. She saw a hand, and a foot, and arms, but not moving how they should be moving. Deep down the drain, a black stringy form emerged from the shadow climbing up the wall with an arachnid dexterity. She saw teeth or eyes glint in the darkness, then screamed and frantically started swimming away from the drain, back toward the shore.

In her panic her competent swimming had become a panicked dog paddle of splashing and frantic head-turning, searching for a direct line to the shore. She looked back and saw a slender dark figure standing on the rim of the drain, with reflective yellow eyes and a pearlescent grin.

Debbie's fear helped her find her focus. She turned her head back to the shore with a new determination. She found her rhythm and swam faster than she ever had. Even faster than the one year in summer camp when she came in number one at the 50-yard freestyle against Jason Slater, but that was a long time ago. Behind her, she heard the splash of a body into the water. She swam on, then felt a bump on her foot, and then a grab as she was pulled under and her hysteria instantly silenced.

~5~

Angelica and Carter stood in the knee-deep water drinking from cans and talking. The light from the shore's campfire was dim but light enough for each of them to make out each other's naked bodies in the titian glow. They liked one another, obviously, and were doing their best to keep eyes locked so as not to contaminate a perfect moment with shame or fear.

In the distance they heard the girls swimming out to the drain, yelling, splashing, and laughing. A distant "Wait Up!" chuckled through the night air.

"The water is causing your makeup to run," Angelica teased Carter.

"Can't always be pretty, unless of course, I was you," he expertly responded.

"Oh, a quick wit," she sarcastically said with added one-handed air quotes, "To add to the guitar playing and good looking face. Should I be worried?". She knew the question was lame but she also knew that they were so far "in it" at this point that no lame question was going to stop "it".

"No," he said, taking another pull from his beer can. "I'm confident with a guitar around my neck, but take that and everything else off and not so much. Success with girls is not my piece de resistance."

As the laughter of the girls in the distance billowed through the evening and the music from the beach bounced off the opposing shore, Angelica stepped closer to Carter. He slipped his hand around her wet, slippery waist and pulled her lips closer to his. She felt the anticipated extra pressure from his naked groin as the side of her hip was pulled into it. They kissed.

Angelica and Carter pulled their faces away from one another and looked off into the darkness upon hearing a yell from out in the lake's wide expanse. "What the fuck are you doing?" Echoed through the cove. They both looked back at the shore and saw the blackened figures of the others standing in front of the campfire staring in the same direction.

"What the fuck was that?" Carter asked.

Angelica just shook her head in ignorance.

A commotion of splashing and yelling then pierced the night and then, silence.

The pair of almost lovers made their way to the shore quickly, as they saw the tall, lanky, naked Two-Bit running up towards the cars. Angelica quickly started putting her clothes on as Carter approached the others.

"What the fuck was that?" Carter again asked, this time to the remaining group.

"They're probably just fucking with us," Brad responded with feigned confidence.

"Ya know, Brad, just because you're a douchebag doesn't mean that other people are?" Tiffany Tiffany responded. "Debbie wouldn't do that." Brad dropped his head in misstep and apologized saying that he was just worried. Tiffany put her hand on his shoulder and they met eyes with a shared look of concern. The two of them went to the shore and started yelling Biscuit's and Debbie's names.

Two-Bit came running back from the cars with a bag in hand. He opened it and pulled out an extra blanket and three flashlights, keeping one and handing the other two to Angelica and Carter. The three shined their flashlights over the murky water.

They passed the beams back and forth across the unbroken surface while the whole group took turns calling the two's names.

"Wha," Two-Bit stuttered, "What is that?" Angelica and Carter matched their flashlights' focus to his.

In the liquid black top of the lake, they saw the top level of Biscuit's face from the nose up, silently glaring at them. The eyes reflected the torches as yellow and as she slowly moved forward her mouth was exposed from the murk, a massive rictus, a grin from ear to ear distorting her face. It was Biscuit, but it was not Biscuit any longer, and she was coming closer.

A Demon Call

A Demon Call

Charles manipulated the duo's massive black car off of the back streets of Kingsport and into the gravel driveway of Abuela Betty's Chophouse. Abuela Betty's Chophouse, known locally as The Pink Bitch, was little more than a run-down diner flanked with big-rig equipped gas pumps. Its fame came in the form of Abuela Betty herself, an old white woman of admittedly no Latin descent that wore gold lamé scenic mu'umu'us and way too much purple eye shadow and silver glitter for a woman of her 70 years, or any age for that matter.

"Abuela Betty's Chophouse," Charles read the name aloud questioningly, then the neon slogan, "Truck Stop Diner to the Stars."

"You want a cupcake, you go to Sugar Plum Fairy's in Arkham, you want a steak and bitter coffee, you go to Abuela Betty's Chophouse." The Professor said.

"Yes, I remember how you feel about this hovel. Does this mean that we want a steak and bitter coffee?" Charles asked.

"Yes it does," The Professor replied, as he answered his ringing cell phone.

Charles navigated the metal mass of a Lincoln between two colossal old rusted trucks.

"Yes Harry," The Professor answered into the phone.

"Kenneth called again," The other end of the phone said. The voice was echoed and tinny as if in a chasm.

"What did you tell him this time?" The Professor questioned with flippant concern.

"What do you think I told him? I told him to fuck off!" Harry proclaimed with frustration.

"Well, Harry, Kenneth is unstable but harmless. Keep him at bay. We'll get around to him eventually."

"I'm not sure about that, Professor. He seemed a little… off?" Harry said.

"Off? How so?"

"Well, he was calm. Normally he's a hot mess, but this time he was, ya know, calm… like creepy calm. God, I hate that little shit. I know I'm trying not to kill anyone, but if I could kill someone, it'd be him." Freddy answered.

"We've all agreed on this. There's only one person we're all willing to kill."

"Right, Professor. Maddie."

The two chuckled a little at the mention of the name of Maddie McGill. No one was really sure why The Professor and Harry both hated Maddie McGill, but it was well known. One day the duo had left on a basic "bag n tag" outing for some artifacts for the Miskatonic Anthropology Department and when they returned home, they hated Maddie McGill.

"We'll get around to her, but as I said, we'll get to Kenneth eventually," The Professor discarded the topic, "but, for now, take the night off, all seems mellow enough."

"Will do, Bossman," Harry hung up the phone.

Harry set his phone down on the nightstand of his room and stretched his arms up in a V while he sat on the edge of his bed. The room was spartan and the walls were concrete.

He stared at the wall for a second. He wore shorts for

sleeping and a thoroughly loved Led Zeppelin Houses of The Holy t-shirt. His arms and legs were smattered with poorly done, oddly spaced, illegible tattoos.

For all the strength that Harry had, Harry was in hiding, proof that there is always someone bigger and badder out there.

Harry had met The professor at least two decades prior. At the time, Harry and a partially ostracised Chatloic priest were on the run from Harry's previous "benefactor", a dark, scary, and possibly demonic man that went by Incubus. Incubus had an uncanny ability to find Harry and the priest no matter where they went until The Professor found four "Mystics". The Four Mystics named not for branding but for the utilitarian purpose that it took four to watch him every hour with some days off for shopping and rec time. Each had the similar ability to keep Harry hidden from Incubus.

Harry stood up and grabbed a towel from the lone shelf in the concrete room and walked to the door. The door was massive and metal, with a big wheel on the front that must be turned to open like a cold-war-era submarine. With little effort, Harry creaked the mass of metal open, revealing a long concrete hallway.

Sitting on the floor in the hallway was a monk, an almost black-skinned man with a shaved head wearing yellow Buddhist Shaolin style robes. He sat, calmly muttering a prayer over a shallow wooden bowl filled almost to the brim with water. As Harry stepped from the room, the monk looked up and said, "Rise and shine it's evening time, Freddy".

"'Sup Thelonious? Wanna take a walk and get some grub?" Freddy asked. "The Bossman says we can take it easy, nothing on the docket."

"Sure," Thelonious said, getting up cautiously making sure not to disturb the water.

Thelonious's was one of The Four Mystics. His real name was Felix Toroama, but he was nicknamed Thelonios after the jazz pianist by Harry for the not so creative reason that he dressed like a monk. He dressed like a monk but was not in the strictest sense an actual monk.

Thelonious was born on the island of Bougainville and had a typical young childhood for the area, a quaint life of fishing, farming, and family, until he turned about five, at which point he gained what he would later refer to as "a tether to cosmic consciousness". Later in life, Thelonious would explain the sensation as his astral body shooting from his body directly towards whatever he was thinking about. Whatever it really was, it caused the young child to rapidly shift between paranoia and panic, to listlessness or even complete catatonia. At that point, with the assistance of The Tribes, the young Thelonious was taken to Aadya Aditih, a Praachi Monastery in Yul where, instead of learning anything of the religion, he was put directly to work controlling his mind.

Upon arrival, the young boy was sat down in front of a rock and told to concentrate on the rock and nothing else for the entire day. The next day and the day after that he was told to do the same, not an easy task for a five-year-old child, but Thelonious immediately found that concentration was better than the chaos that he was experiencing before.

Over the years he slowly learned to split his concentration allowing him to briefly focus on other things. In his twenties, once he became stable at multiple concentrations, he was sent to live with The Professor in a halfway house situation, which is where several of his other skills were discovered, one of which was his ability to hide Harry's presence from Incubus.

Harry and Thelonious continued down the institutional concrete hallway, their affable voices slapping off the dense walls as they chatted like school friends. At the end of the hallway, they came to a narrow set of metal stairs. At the top, a wooden hatch. Once opened they went up and through, into the living room of the massive and ornate home of Professor Johnathan Whateley.

You Keep
Your Phone On
and You Run

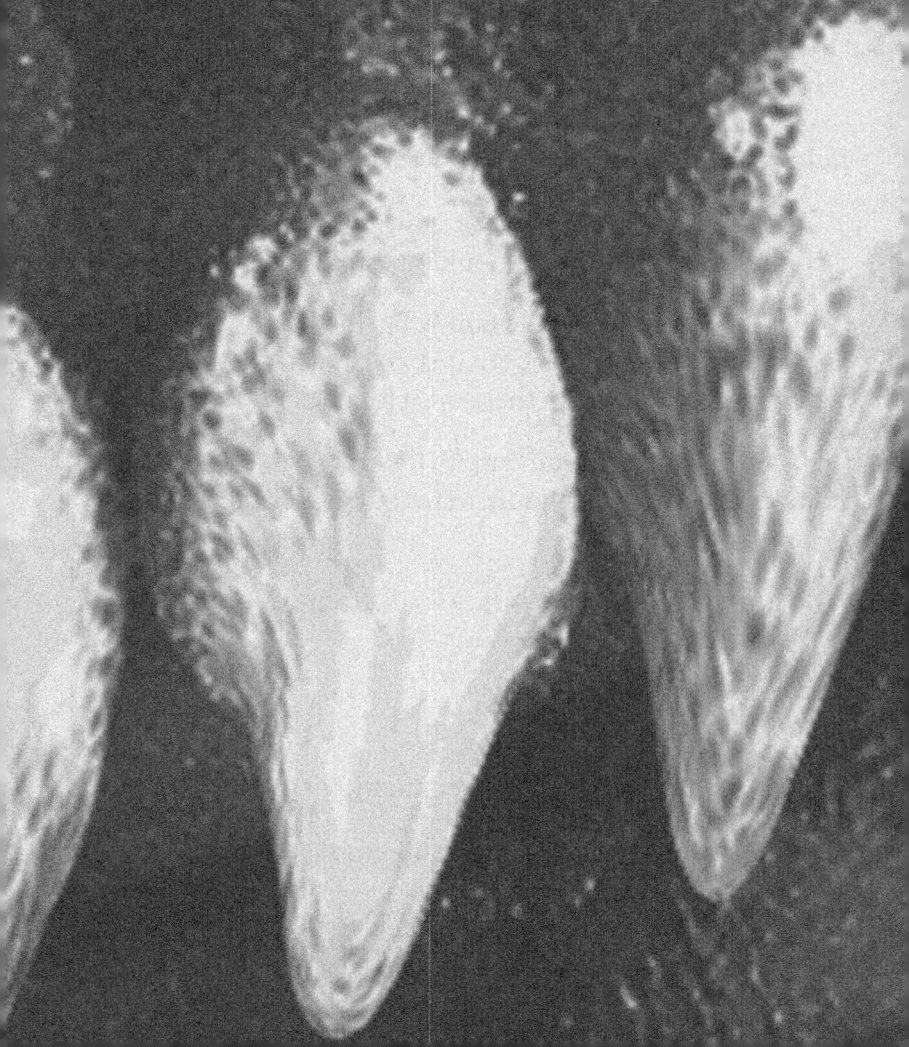

You Keep Your Phone On and You Run

The shore was silent as the group was mesmerized by the reflective eyes that peered back at them from the surface of the water. Without breaking the locked gaze, Angelica reached in her pocket and pulled out her phone, slowly, avoiding any sudden movements. Her eyes still focused on the water, she dialed her father and piecemealed the phone up to her ear while simultaneously clicking the volume as low as she'd be able to hear with her thumb.

Her father answered, "Hello, Honey, I didn't expect to hear from you so soon. Charles and I are getting a steak at our old hidey-haunt, Abuela Betty's."

"That's great, Dad. Um, just a quick question, what do I do again if I run into a demon looking thing?" she quietly asked.

"Finally, interested in the family business huh? Or just showing off to your music friends? Well, what kinda demon looking thing? Ya know, there are a lot of 'em out there."

"I can't rightly say, Dad, but it's looking at me right now and it looks very hungry," she answered, the panic in her voice becoming obvious.

"Are you still in Bolton?" he asked abruptly.

"Yes," she whispered.

"And a demon is staring at you?"

"Yes," she repeated even more quietly.

"Is your phone charged?" Her father asked.

Confused, she stole a glance at the screen of the phone; 80%. Again, she replied, "Yes."

"You keep your phone on and you run," he said emphatically.

"What?" she asked, her voice quivering.

"Keep your phone powered on and keep it on your person so we can find you and then run, as fast and as far as you can."

"Um, okay," Angelica hung up the phone and in a mix of terrified trembling and Millenial habit, slipped the phone back into her pocket.

Carter quietly whispered to her. "What did he say?"

"He said to run."

"Fuck," he mumbled beneath his breath, "Somehow I thought he was going to say that."

Behind them, they heard rustling and turned and saw the others already running off through the darkness, up the dunes of sand, toward the cars.

Then, a splash from the water as they simultaneously turned back to the creature to see the body of Debbie Debbie splash in the wet sand at their feet, spraying blood and lakewater up at them.

The eyes and mouth of the body were gaping open and stared up at them in lifeless horror, its once petite frame a confusion of bent limbs and bloody skin.

"Run!" Carter yelled, pushing Angelica ahead of him as they rushed toward the parking lot, cutting through the sand and the darkness.

Arriving at the cars, they found the rest of the group getting dressed in whatever they had or whatever they could find. Carter grabbed clothes and did the same.

"What the fuck man," Brad whimpered, his face ghostly white with terror, eerily accentuated by the hum of the fluorescent parking lot lights, "What the fuck was that? Was that Biscuit? It fucking looked like Biscuit!"

"Calm down and get in the car," Angelica said to him.

Brad prepared to continue with his panicked outrage when the atmosphere took on an even more creepy quiet. Each of them felt a shiver in their spines and bodywide goosebumps. Then a sound cut through the silence, an audible buzzsaw vibration, a metallic sustained reverberation. The lights of the parking lot, the car, the flashlights, all the lights flickered, then died at the same moment the sound stopped.

Two-Bit hopped in the car and turned the key, "Fuck! Fuck! Fuck!" He stuck his head out the side, "Nothing. It's dead".

After some quick, hysterical conversation, it was agreed that they'd continue running to the market they had passed on the way here. They grabbed the flares they could find by the moon's light and took one last survey of the water.

In the distance, the only light was the dim glow of their shore fire, orange against the black backdrop. Slowly, another glow emerged. The smooth glass of the lake top started to glint with a pale green hue. The green-lit surface of the lake broke as Biscuit's bluish-pale body slowly started walking to the shore. In the water, darker twists of green, while on top, flushes of dark blue, red, and purple algae massed, bloomed, then floated away in dead black clumps. Her feet stepped onto the sandy shore, each footprint spawning a small unnatural garden of unearthly vines and thorned flowers that spread and died. She walked toward them, looking directly at them. With each step, the same flush of growth, so vibrant and colorful with otherworldly plant life, growing, only die to a charred black moments later. With each step, she stood in abundant life and left a trail of death as she started walking toward the dark parking lot.

Down the Drain, Down the Drain

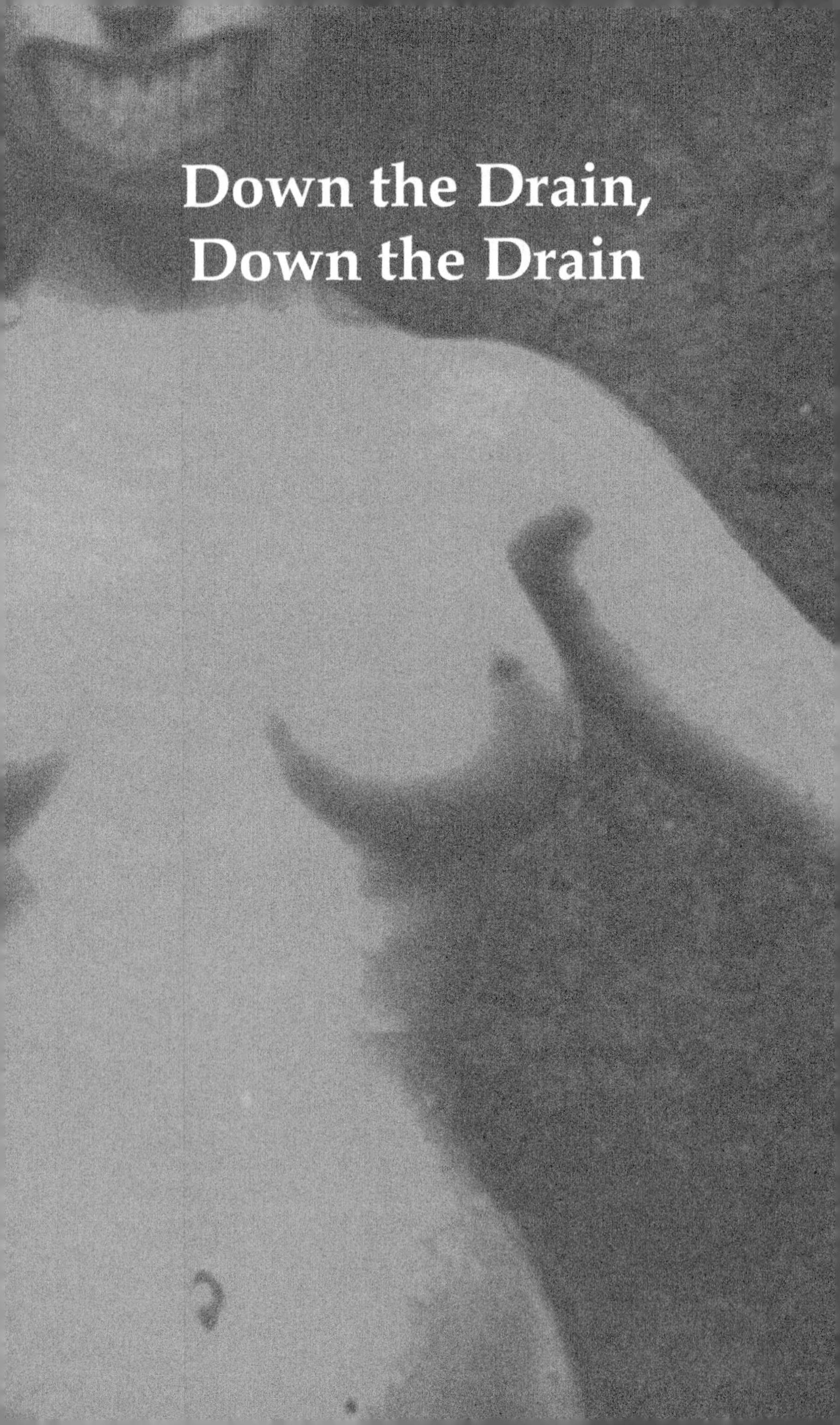

Down the Drain, Down the Drain

Stunned by the sight before them, the remaining quintet stood in the parking lot as the blueish-green, corpselike body of what was once their friend walked toward them from the water. Even from the long-distance, they could make out the yellow reflection in her eyes and glowing growth and death at her feet, but mostly they could make out her smile. A smile so large that it distorted her face and warped her lips and teeth into a terrifying rictus.

"We have to get out of here," Angelica murmured, "We have to keep moving."

Glossy, tearful eye-contact was made among the group as they took their supplies and turned and ran toward the market at the edge of town. Deep into the darkness, they ran, trying not to look back, trying not to talk, trying not to cry, trying not to think, but Angelica did.

For the first time in as long as she could remember she hoped that her dad would find her, that he would come to her rescue. He hadn't been there for her much. Maybe that wasn't fair. He had been there, just maybe not in the ways that she wanted or needed him to be. He was a deeply critical man and that can leave scars on a child, driving the course of their lives toward self-destruction, or at least counseling.

For all of his belittling commentary and biting wit, he was there. Most of the time she felt that he was just there to tell her what she was doing wrong, tell her she had to be better, inform her of all of his unattainable expectations and hopelessly lofty goals. Not his goals for himself, but his goals for her. She had come to a point of forgiveness, however, she'd hit the age a while ago where she had become aware that his drive for her success was his weaknesses in himself, that his words to her were forgotten interpretations of his father's words to him. He didn't mean it, but how often it is that we hold grudges and carry scars from inflictions that were not malicious. Probably most of them, if not all?

As she ran, she told herself that if there was a part of her that did not forgive him, if he saved her, she would forgive it.

As she ran, she told herself that if there is a part of him that she has refused to understand, if he saved her, she would try harder.

As she ran, she remembered times when he was and was not there. He was there when he had to be. Those times that threaten a parent's safety, threaten a parent's reputation. Times like her saxophone recital and the meeting with the principal that followed due to her pulling down the pants and underwear of Geoffery Taylor in the ninth grade. It was the first penis she had ever seen in person and up until now, the memory was burned into the back of her mind. Now, most of the memory was gone. What was once a memory that was hers, a defining memory of her youth, was now just a memory of when her dad was there to bail her out.

But there were times when he was there when she did need him and she didn't know it. At the time they too were a source of frustration, a source of embarrassment. Like in tenth grade when she snuck out of the house and got way too drunk at Jennifer Cooly's house when Jennifer's mom was out of town. The house was full of drunk boys and girls. Angelica had imbibed so much that she was throwing up uncontrollably on the back porch as the other kids laughed and pointed. Her dad came storming in and picked her up completely, even with his slight frame, carried her to the car, and took her home. It was the first time she realized that he was tracking her phone, but he also held her hair away from her face while she expelled what alcohol was left in her system and then made her a sandwich.

And, of course, he was there when her mom died.

It's sometimes shocking how relativity comes into play, such as the comparison of a spoiled rich girl who doesn't want to be embarrassed by her dad and a girl from a third world country that has to do unspeakable things just to eat at the same age. She never had a relative moment to truly put things into perspective, until now. If he came, if he dropped everything and saved her from this smiling face of evil that literally wanted to consume her, the needle would be shoved. It would be shoved so far to one side that everything he ever did or did not do that hurt her would be minuscule in comparison.

Next to her, there was a crack and a sizzle as Carter ignited one of the flares. The light both terrified and comforted her. Comfort that she could see, terror of what she might see.

"It's not far. There'll be a phone," Carter said through heavy panting to the left of her. Left of Carter she could hear the footfalls and whimpering of Brad, to her right she saw the eyes of Tiffany, wild with fear, and beyond that, the stone-faced look on TwoBits face.

Brad fell to his knees sobbing as the group stopped.

"Get up!" Carter yelled, attempting to convey compassion, but expressing only panic.

"What's the point?" Brad moaned into his hands.

"We have to keep moving," Tiffany begged, crawling under Brad's arm trying to help him up.

Carter grabbed his other arm and threw it over his shoulder and helped get Brad to his feet, "Come on, man. I'll help you, but we have to keep moving."

"On, shit," Angelica whispered as she noticed and pointed at a faint green glow in the tree line next to them. Looking up, they could see the sharp silhouettes of the trees in the starlight expanding and bending, the ominous creek of the growth and death of the trees cutting the silence, a subtle sound made deafening by the fear and stillness surrounding.

"Fuck, fuck, fuck," TwoBit repeated as he fumbled through his bag and found the other flare. He cracked off the striker cap doubling the orange glow as they all looked into the blackness around them. "Get him the fuck up and let's keep going," he continued, attempting to sound commanding.

"Deb's dead," was Brad's only response.

"I know she's fucking dead and we'll all be fucking dead too if we don't start moving you fucking pussy!" TwoBit yelled at Brad, darting his eyes back and forth at the group in front of him. "Fucking leave his ass, we have to go!"

"I'm not leaving him," Carter said to TwoBit.

"You're such a bleeding heart pussy, you fucking pussy," TwoBit now directed at Carter, "your sensitive, shy bullshit might work at the fucking warehouse or some shithole coffee shop, but that shit ain't gonna keep you alive now! Now, fucking move!"

"How is this helping?" Angelica asked.

"Fuck you too, you fucking talentless hack!"

"Woah man, chill out," Carter said, finding some assertiveness.

46

"Look who got a backbone," TwoBit continued as the group just watched his anger fueled breakdown, the anger and fear in his face exaggerated by the whipping orange sulfuric light sources against the blackest black. A black so dark all depth to it is gone, except...

From behind TwoBit a feature broke the blackness. Two yellow eyes peering through the darkness. The eyes moved quickly, but the adrenaline of fear allowed every second to seem like minutes as Angelica watched powerlessly. A sharp nose cut through the dark beneath the eyes and then below that, the awful, dreadful smile of teeth and blood. Large triangular fangs and curled lips moved toward the unexpecting TwoBit. Through the darkness, an orange-lit cerulean hand with black claws and blood splatter rose above him.

As protracted as the previous moments were the next came in stark contrast. As Angelica looked on, the clawed hand came immediately down from behind, over TwoBit's head to his chin, and then quickly raked up his face slashing along the way until sticking in his eye sockets. Angelica's shouldered then startled with the popping sound and the gush of blood from TwoBit's face and eyes.

TwoBit dropped the flare as his body was ripped back into the vertical sea of darkness.

"No!" Angelica yelled, scrambling forward and grabbing the flare, then holding it as far out as she could to try to see in the black.

"There!" Tiffany howled, pointing off into the darkness.

Angelica threw the flare in the pointed direction. In the flarelight they saw the naked pale body of Biscuit hunched over the still corpse of TwoBit as she used her neck and razor teeth to rip chunks of flesh from his face.

"Go… Now!" Angelica wailed as the remaining four ran in the opposite direction from the gore. Ahead, far down the road, they saw a lone streetlight in the darkness illuminating the small roadside market.

Their adrenaline did its job. What seemed like an insurmountable distance passed in a moment as they approached the market.

The market, called T-Birds, was one of those old highway stores that only saw business during the tourism months. It was probably buzzing when the road was a highway, but when the new freeway was put in years ago, it was relegated to a drinks and ice stop on the way to the lake. At that moment, to Angelica, it was a haven, a fortress, a castle glowing with hope under its lone streetlight.

They ran to the locked door of T-Birds and, with a new found lust for life or vengeance, Brad immediately punched through the glass, reached through, and unlocked the door. Throwing the flares into the street, they scrambled inside.

Inside the store was lit with crosshairs of shadow from the windows, flares, and the streetlight. They huddled in a pile at the back of the store, attempting to catch their breath and their sanity.

Angelica felt her heart skip a beat as she noticed the hairs on the back of her neck stand on end. Again the thunderous metallic sound resonated through the night rattling the store's windows and extinguishing the streetlight.

They held each other in the darkness, wondering what to do next.

End of the Road

End of the Road

"Daniel has really shaped up," Denise thought as she comfortably gripped the steering wheel and lazily eyed the headlight illuminated road while listening to her son, Daniel, talk about how his school is going.

"…Yeah, I really like my roommates, and my teachers seem cool, so far. Mostly, I just like being out of the house. Not that I want away from you and Dad, it's just nice to be in charge." he said.

It's amazing, less than a year ago they were not sure he'd even be going to college. He had the grades and, thanks to Denise and her husband's low tax bracket, all the expenses were practically covered. It was hard for Denise to conceive that six months ago they were picking him up at the police station and now they were picking him up from college, and Servi Deorum Chatloic even.

It was more of a drive to see him than Denise would prefer, and they ended up having to wait in line too long checking out of student housing. Now it was getting late, well passt midnight, but Ipswitch was right up the road and they would finally be home. "At least they have time to catch up and I can get to know the new him better," she thought. "Like, his new interest in growing up, in programming, and apparently this new electronic music, synthrave, or wave, or something like that."

Denise saw a faint yellow glow from the dash, "Darnit, Looks like we're gonna have to stop and get gas. Tell me if you see anything, Daniel."

"No worries, I could use a soda," he responded.

Daniel put his arm and flat hand out the window and allowed his hand to be whipped up and down by the rushing air.

Up ahead, in the beams of the headlights was a green reflection. As it got closer the highway sign became legible, "Bolton 5 MILES".

Daniel spoke up, "Bolton, 5 Miles, Mom."

"Do you think they'll have gas?"

"As a man of the world now, I have learned one thing, Mom. If a town has a name, it has a gas station."

"Yeah, I guess that's true, but will it be open?"

"Mom, even hicks have technology now. We'll be able to swipe the card and pump ourselves."

"Let's hope so."

"They will."

"So have you met any nice girls at college?" she asked. "Or are nice girls even what you're interested in?"

"Are you asking me if I'm gay or are you asking if I'm into kegger sluts?" Daniel asked.

Denise was a little taken aback by the casual use of the term "kegger sluts" from her son, but she tried to brush off the awkwardness and move on, "I was thinking a little more down the lines of are you pursuing girls at this point, or only interested in school and your future, but sure, I'll bite, are you gay or into kegger… sluts?"

"No, Mom, I'm not gay, and yes, I would like a nice girl. I've met a few, but nothing has gone anywhere. Just the usual."

Again, Denise was confused as to if 'the usual' meant flirty banter or drunken sex. "Why is this so confusing?" she thought. "I was young once. It wasn't even that long ago. What is it about getting older? When I did those things as a kid it was a part of getting smarter and growing up, but now, when my kid may be doing them, I view it as the bane of society and how we have lost our way."

"I'm guessing from your quietness, Mom, that you're thinking about giving me the sex talk, yet again, so, no, I am not having sex with any of them."

"I wasn't thinking that!" she lied.

"Whatever, Mom. I know you better than you know me. While I've been growing up and changing for nineteen years, you've been the same consistent mom."

While there was some truth to what he was saying, she still didn't like it. "I've changed!"

"Well, yeah I guess so. You drink less wine and read more books at night."

"See, I have changed," she said with sarcastic pride.

"Looks like there is a gas station coming up, Mom," Daniel said with a point toward the windshield.

Ahead they saw the dim lights of a gas station first and then a small local store. She pulled up to the pumps hoping that they were open, or at least able to pump gas. She looked at the gas station with disappointment, noticing that it was dark, but found some relief when she saw LED lights of the pay terminals on the pumps, "Oh, thank God." She stopped at one of the pumps and the duo got out of the car.

"This is, even more, the middle nowhere than Ipswitch,"

Daniel stated, obviously, slamming the car door behind him. "What a dump."

"Daniel, I'm sure it's a nice little town."

Daniel ignored the politeness of his mother, "There's a soda machine. Want anything?"

"No, I'll pump the gas, just hurry up. I want to get home and get to bed. I have to work in the morning and it's already very late," she said to him.

"Yup," he responded.

Daniel strutted over to the red glowing soda machine sitting in front of the darkened gas station. He looked up as he went, chest puffing out in awkward teenage confidence, noticing the tall tree points silhouetted in front of the starry night. In a worldly effort, he tried to think something profound about the view but was quickly distracted back toward the vending machine.

He stepped up the curb and to the machine. "Coke, Diet, Sprite," he prattled off to himself while he dug in his pockets for some bills. At the bottom of his left pocket, he found a wad of crumpled one-dollar bills. He straightened two of them out on the corner of the vending machine and slid them into the money slot. He took a pointless moment to make his choice, knowing that he would pick the same one he always does. He bumped his fist on the bright red button indicating Coke. There was a whizzing sound, and a clunk, and then, nothing.

"Fuuuuck," he exhaled to himself, his chin falling to his chest. Then, as teen boys often do, he decided to fix it by giving it a solid smack or kick. He looked to his right to see if he could get away with this assault of the dispenser and saw literally nothing, nothing but the dark road they came in on. He looked to the left and saw the dark market, but not entirely dark. There was a waving light in one of the windows. "Is that a lighter?" he questioned to himself.

In the dim window across the parking lot, he could see a lighter waving back and forth and behind it, several hands waving. Are they waving him away? Are they waving him closer? "Fucking hick tweakers," he said to himself with contempt.

He started walking back to the pumps, "Mom, the stupid machine is busted, and there're some tweakers in the next building trying to get our attention."

"What?" Denise said, looking up while still gripping the pump handle. In the window of the store, she saw the same thing, a lighter and several hands waving. They appeared to be waving frantically, "Do they need help?" she said, puzzled.

"Who cares?" Daniel rhetorically responded.

"We care, Daniel. That's who cares," she said with disappointment in her voice.

"Fine, I'll check it out," the teen said with a huff and immediately started making his way toward the store.

"Daniel, wait!" she called to him.

Daniel didn't stop. Why on earth would she have expected him to? He hasn't been one for listening up until now, and she can't see any reason why he'd start at nineteen.

As the boy approached, he could tell that the people inside were yelling.

As he got within yards of the window he could make out a

face, a face with red hair and light skin. A face that would be kinda pretty if it wasn't completely consumed with terror. He could finally make out the words she was yelling. "Run, get the fuck out of here! Don't come here! Get in your car and call for help, you dumb shit!"

The boy looked on in shock. While being nineteen makes one feel like they can take on the world, in reality, at nineteen few have taken on much, and Daniel was not the exception. He was frozen in confusion.

"Fuck, fuck, fuck! Behind you! Behind you!" The would-be-pretty girl yelled at him. He turned around to his mother. He saw her, pumping gas, looking at him in bewilderment, the pumps, the car, and, behind the car, he saw another girl. A naked girl with pale, almost blue skin, with a body that was bruised, a body that was plump while also emaciated, a corpse, a corpse with a hideous smile that conveyed nothing but hunger.

"Mom!" he yelled running toward his mother. "Look out!"

She looked to her left and right, then shrugged her shoulders looking back at him with confusion. At that moment she registered the fear on her son's face. A twisted look of terror that she had never seen before, but immediately deciphered that whatever was causing that look of terror was right behind her. She quickly turned with only enough time to register the rictus, the awful, tooth-filled smile, and hear a metallic burning sound as the lights of the station went out with a sizzle.

Denise threw up her free hand in defense as the corpse grabbed her by the wrist and side of her neck and then flexed. With a wet pop and a meaty tear, her arm was ripped from the socket by the walking horror and the arm was thrown over its shoulder, discarded as it moved in for the main course.

The fang-filled maw bore down on her neck, slicing through the meat and bone like massive razor blades. Daniel watched as the creature ripped its head back pulling the meat with it leaving an almost comical shark bite in his mother's body.

"Noooo!" he cried as he stumbled back, falling to the ground on his hands and butt, knees up, unable to stop gawking at the horror before him in the starlight.

The creature threw the mother's body to the side and leapt like a cat onto the hood of the car, licking its blood-stained hand.

"No," Daniel whimpered.

The creature pounced upon the boy, dragging its jaw from his belly to his neck, ripping his insides open, exposing his guts. Daniel felt nothing. He just looked down at the creature laying over him as she, almost lovingly, stared at his gaping wound, staring at her next meal.

The Other Side of the Call

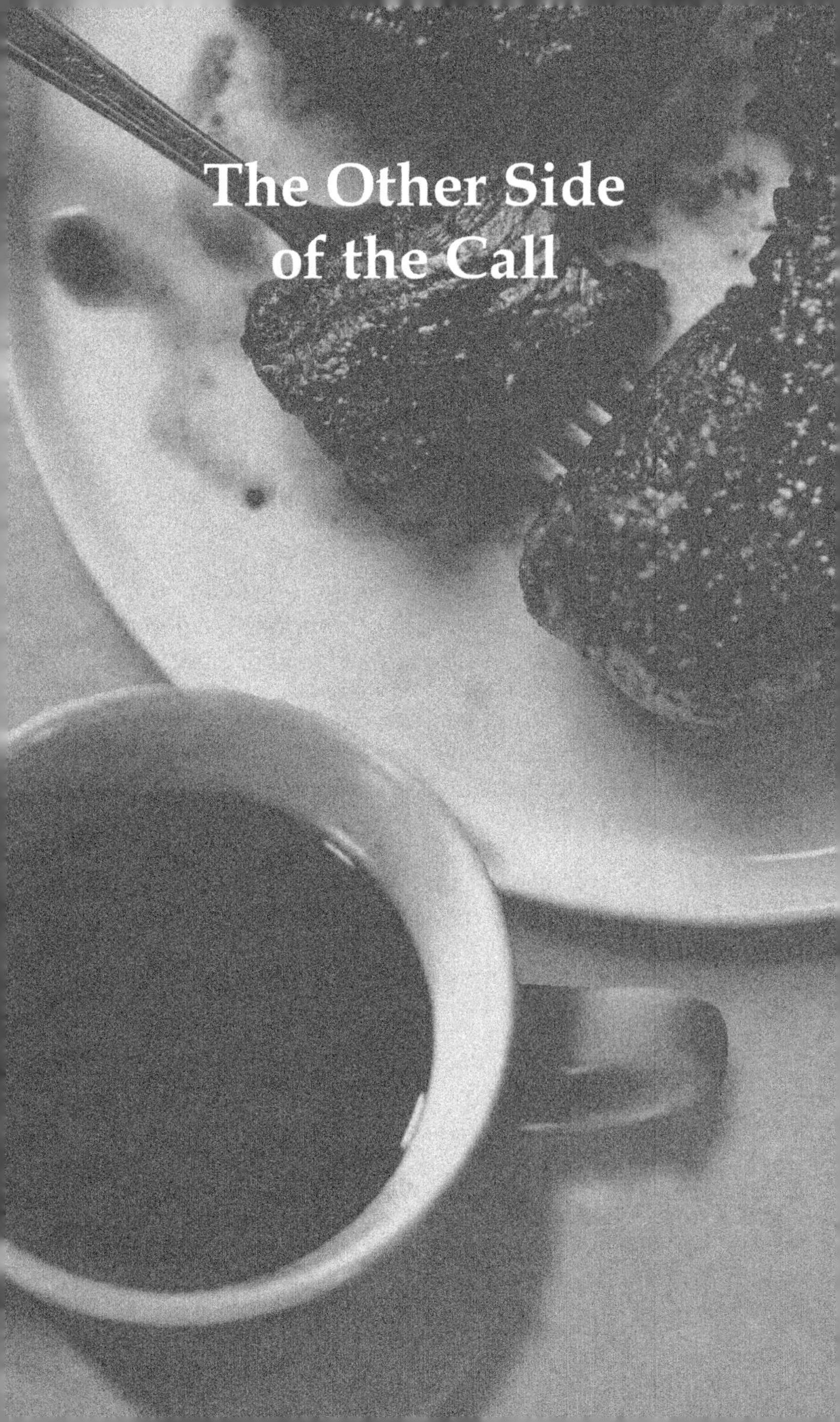

The Other Side of the Call

Two Hours Earlier

Professor Johnathan Whateley and his husband Charles sat over disturbingly raw steaks at Abuela Betty's Chophouse. The wafting of the near raw meat and the black bitter coffee filled The Professor with nostalgia for simpler times. Charles was unfazed by the slightly charred gore before him, other than thinking, "Next time, I chose the restaurant".

"What is it about this place?" Charles asked with a puzzlement bordering on concern. "I mean, it's a wreck. There is no way it's sanitary"

"All meat is sanitary if you burn the outside and nothing grows in bitter coffee," The Professor responded, scooping up a chunk and getting it in his mouth before it dripped.

"Neither of those things are true," Charles pointlessly pointed out as he began to slice his own steak while pleasantly nodding his head to the ridiculous muzak version of some eighties song.

"Is that Johnny?" a woman from across the restaurant called. Charles looked up to see a woman coming over.

"What have we here, Johnny?" Charles asked The Professor under his breath.

The Professor looked up from his steak, "What, huh?"

Charles nodded his head in the direction of the woman.

"It is you!" she cried and sped up her approach.

Her walk couldn't be described as a waddle, but, at the same time, it couldn't really be described as a walk either, more the rolling and shifting of fat pouches and bones. She was an older woman in an odd, sparkling muumuu, with wild hair, and a wilder smile. Charles recognized her from the picture coming in. This was Abeula Betty.

She approached the table. "How are you boys doing? Haven't seen you in these parts for some time Johnny?" She half asked, "Hope you been missing me as much as I've been missing you," she followed with a wink.

"I always miss your cooking, darlin'. Best steaks in the greater Arkham area," The Professor said.

"It's not those steaks I was hoping you were missn'," she flirted with a raise of her purple-tinted eyebrows.

"Yes, John, it's not those steaks she was talking about," Charles said, looking The Professor right in the eye with a smirk.

"And who's your friend here?" Betty asked with a smile.

"This pissy queen is Charles, he's my husband," The Professor said dropping another chunk of meat in his mouth, knowing that the realization of him having a husband would at least put an end to part of the excruciating conversation.

"Well, that explains a lot," she realized with a little disappointment.

Charles stood up and put out his hand in greeting, "Miss Betty." Charles easily stood a foot taller than her and was two or three times her width at the shoulders.

"You're a big one ain't ya? Can't compete with you, sweety. You are one glorious piece of man meat." she cackled.

Charles glanced down at the raw steak on his plate. "Well, I do appreciate your expertise."

"Ooooo and funny! Johnny, you got a good one here. Now listen, you boy's food is on ol' Betty tonight, and don't let yourself be strangers." She said to The Professor, and then turned to Charles, "And if you're family with Johnny, you're family with me, so I hope to see you more often too."

"Yes, Ma'am," Charles acknowledged with a wink, as she moved on to another table, knowing the people at that one too. Charles returned to his meal and started quietly eating with a smile.

"I suppose you want to know a back story," The Professor mumbled out through another bite of meat.

"Oh no. I'd just assume let this one fester and bring it up at the least opportune time."

"Great," The professor murmured, fumbling for the ringing phone in his pocket.

Happy to be out of the fire for the moment, he saw that the call was coming from Angelica and he answered. "Hello, Honey, I didn't expect to hear from you so soon. Charles and I are getting a steak at our old hidey-haunt, Abuela Betty's."

"That's great, Dad. Um, just a quick question, what do I do again if I run into a demon looking thing?" she quietly asked through the phone.

"Finally, interested in the family business huh? Or just showing off to your music friends? Well, what kinda demon looking thing? Ya know, there are a lot of 'em out there." He said to Angelica as he saw Charles roll his eyes at him. The Professor shrugged and waved Charles quiet with his free hand.

"I can't rightly say, Dad, but it's looking at me right now and it looks very hungry," the panic in her voice had become obvious.

"Are you still in Bolton?" he asked with a new seriousness that perked up Charle's ears.

"Yes," she whispered.

"And a demon is staring at you?"

"Yes," she repeated even more quietly.

"Is your phone charged?" The Professor asked.

There was a short pause and then Angelica answered, "Yes."

"Keep your phone on you and run," he ordered. At this order into the phone, Charles got in his pocket and dropped several twenties on the table, and started getting up.

"What?" she asked, her voice quivering.

"Keep your phone powered on and keep it on your person so we can find you and then run, as fast and as far as you can."

"Um, okay," Angelica said and then hung up the phone.

"Honey…?" The Professor said into the phone and then realized that the conversation had ended.

Standing over The Professor, Charles asked, "What is it?". The Professor just looked forward. "What is it, John?" Charles repeated.

"It must be the goo," The Professor said flatly.

"And Angel?" Charles demanded.

"From what I can tell, it's not her," he answered getting up and grabbing his jacket, "but it might be hunting her."

The two made their way toward the door, ignoring the waving Betty. "Which location? Bolton?" Charles inquired.

"Bolton."

"Good," Charles stated as they picked up the pace through the parking lot of the chophouse toward the Lincoln.

Confused, looking at Charles as they moved, The Professor asked, "Good? Why good?"

When they got to the car, Charles popped open the trunk and handed a bag to The Professor. "While that fissure is ancient and sure to be powerful, it was only opened for a moment. The legend said that it was a single droplet." Charles grabbed a large briefcase from the trunk and threw it in the passenger seat.

The Professor went to get in the passenger side.

"Where do you think you're going?" Charles asked authoritatively.

"To get Angelica."

"No," Charles grabbed the phone, still in The Professor's hand and tapped a red app, and handed it back to him. "Harry is on his way. When he gets here, John, you will direct him to us while I hold it off."

"No way, Charles! I'm coming!"

"No you're not," Charles said getting in the driver's seat, closing the door, and firing up the engine.

"She's my daughter, Charles."

"She's our daughter, John, and we've discussed this sort of

situation. This is the best way. This is what we agreed upon."
Charles didn't wait for an answer and drove away with a
roar of the engine, leaving The Professor slack-jawed in the
parking lot.

"But, we didn't agree! You just told me this was how it
would go and I wouldn't have a choice!" The Professor yelled
after the car, watching the black Continental pick up speed
and rev off into the night.

You Can't
Burn a Demon

You Can't Burn a Demon

Angelica, Carter, Tiffany, and Brad scoured T-Birds market looking for anything they could use for defense.

"What the hell do you fight a demon with?" Brad said, frantically knocking items off shelves.

"Booze!" Carter shouted.

"Great, what are we gonna do? Party with it?" Brad patronized.

"No, dumbass. We're gonna burn it." Carter responded holding two gallons of Everclear.

"Good idea," Angelica said, running over and grabbing bottles as well.

Correcting them, Brad said "No, not a good idea. You said it's a demon. Like hellfire and shit. You can't burn a demon!"

"It's just a fucking word I used. I don't know if it's a demon, but I do know that most things burn," Angelica answered, grabbing a gaudy Lake Hali tourist t-shirt and attempted to rip it.

"Fuck," Brad surrendered and helped Angelica rip the shirt into strips.

"Tiff, grab some lighters," Carter asked, pointing to the cigarettes behind the counter.

Beams of halogen light poured through the store's windows, Brad noticed and ran to a side window looking out at the gas station next door, "It's a car!" he yelled.

At Brad's yell, Angelica looked up from shoving rips of cloth into Everclear bottles and saw the gaunt silhouette of the creature move past the front window in the direction of the lights, a blue blur that sent chills down her spine.

"Fuck, that thing is moving toward them," she said as she, Carter, and Tiffany joined brad at the window.

Out of the window, they could see a middle-aged woman and a young man getting out of a car at one of the gas pumps. The woman started pumping gas as the young man started walking toward the station's building.

"There is still some power over there," Tiffany noted. "We have to tell them to get out of there."

Brad yelled out the window, "Hey, you dumb shits! You need to get the fuck out of here!"

Tiffany started waving a lighter in the window, trying to get the people's attention as the rest of the group joined in, yelling to the strangers at the gas station to leave and get help.

After a few moments, the young man noticed the group warning him. He walked back toward the woman.

"He saw us!" Tiffany yelled in excitement.

"Oh, thank god," Angelica muttered.

Her relief was broken when Carter announced that the young man was coming back toward them. The fervor rose again as the quartet started screaming and yelling at the guy as he continued moving closer to them.

As he got closer Angelica realizes that he was just a teen, a teen that of course had no idea what waited for him in the woods. He got close enough that he could hear and made eye contact with her.

"Run, get the fuck out of here! Don't come here! Get in your car and call for help, you dumb shit!" Angelica screamed at him. Behind the boy was what Angelica assumed to be his mother, and behind her, the blue twisted form of Biscuit.

"Fuck, fuck, fuck! Behind you! Behind you!" She screamed again pointing behind the boy.

The boy turned. He took a moment to register the horror behind the woman and he started running toward her yelling, "Mom!".

It was too late. With a lightning-fast bite and pull the creature that was once Biscuit practically ripped the woman in half, leapt on the car, and stared down her new prey as the lights at the station went out. The boy stumbled back falling down in the darkness as the hideous blue corpse descended upon him, eviscerating him in a moment.

Out of instinct, all four of the spectators dropped to the floor of the store, out of sight of the window.

After a few moments of silence, Angelica spoke, "We have to fight. We don't have a choice."

"How the hell are we supposed to beat that thing?" Tiffany asked.

"It doesn't matter," Angelica responded. "It's either die on our feet or die on our backs. My father will send Charles. My father will send Harry."

"Who the hell are Charles and Harry?" Brad asked.

"Charles is my Dad's husband… my stepdad, and Harry is, like on the run or something, but he's like a warrior tough guy. They will help us. They deal with this sorta thing" She told him, half telling herself as well.

"Fucking great. Some gay dude and a con on the lamb. That's what we're waiting for?" Brad mumbled.

Normally, Angelica would have taken offense to the statement, but now it seemed of little importance and all she said was, "We have to fight."

"Ok then, we fight." Carter chimed in standing up and moving toward the bottles of Everclear, their do-it-yourself arsenal of Molotov cocktails.

They each grabbed two of the incendiary devices and slowly approached the door, feet numb and legs of jelly. Tiffany took her lighter and lit each of the rags sticking out of the bottles.

Angelica took the lead, "Listen I know we're all scared, but we're in a wooden building. When we do this we have to go outside to her. We can't mess this up or we'll burn down our own fort. Got it?" She made sure to make eye contact with each and made sure that it was responded with a nod.

Angelica pinched one of the Molotov cocktails in her armpit and twisted the door handle and pulled it in just enough to get the toe of her shoe between it and the frame. She returned the weapon to her hand and made eye contact again, then she swung the door open with her foot.

The four stood in the doorway, illuminated by the flame of each bottle. In front of them was the dark stretch of the two lanes of the highway. On the other side of the highway, perched atop a high concrete retaining wall was the creature. Its eyes glinted at them, its teeth barely visible yet undeniably there.

The creature's head dropped low as her shoulders rose up and that hideous metallic buzz saw noise cut through the night air again, rattling the windows of the store and blowing a hot breeze across the group's faces. In fear, they all looked down to get reassured that the rags in their bombs were still burning, to each one's relief they were.

"Good ol' Everclear," Brad said.

The creature dropped the ten or so feet from the top of the retaining wall landing unphased on the far shoulder of the highway, then started walking toward the store. As she approached the intention in her eyes was clear, as if they needed to be reminded. Her blood-stained tongue outlined the ridges of her razor teeth and smile.

"Wait until she's a little closer," Angelica ordered, as she stepped forward out of the doorway and into the parking lot of the store. The others reluctantly followed her, "Hold," she commanded. As the creature approached, she took another step closer followed by the terrified trio behind her.

"Hold," she repeated as much to herself as to her battalion.

With the creature just twenty feet away she yelled, "Now!" and let the first of the Molotov cocktails fly, followed by the other and then the rest from the group. The glass bottles soared through the air in seeming slow motion. The first bottle hit the ground as the liquid spread around the demonic girl's feet. There was a moment of fear, a fear of failure, a fear that the fire did not start. Shoulders dropped in slight repose as the liquid glowed blue for a second and then exploded with the impact of the following bottles into a burst of flame running like rivers across the highway. The creature was completely engulfed. Billows of hot wind blew across them.

"Yes!" Carter cried, arms up in victory.

Down the highway, they heard a screeching of tires and saw headlights coming toward them at a high rate of speed.

"It's my dad's car!" Angelica sobbed.

They looked at their rescue coming toward them quickly, a solid black old beast of a car.

"Oh, fuck me," Tiffany said with a whine of defeat as the others looked to see.

The body of Biscuit was emerging, unphased from the flame. With that horrible buzzsaw sound and gust of air, the flames at her feet were pushed away as she continued her path toward them.

Charles,
Down the Drain

Charles, Down the Drain

The black Lincoln Continental barreled down the road towards Bolton, the sound of the roaring engine deafening Charles as he glanced at an open briefcase with a built-in military-grade laptop in the passenger seat. On the screen, a map and a marker, the map was of the Bolton area, the marker was Angelica, and she was right up ahead.

The area seemed to be a never-ending road of curves with just more trees past every turn jetting up in the darkness casting strobing shadows and demanding that Charles slow his speed every few feet, but this turn was different. As Charles rounded it he saw a blazing fire in the middle of the street, and in the middle, a silhouette. It was the shape of a woman, but not a woman, a creature, the creature. To the right of the inferno, he saw a group of four young people but zeroed in on only one of the faces. It is Angelica and she looked more terrified than he had ever seen her before. She looked over at him and from her gaze alone he could tell that the thing in the flames had to die.

Straightening out of the turn, he saw what appeared to be a gust of air from the center of the blaze that extinguished most of the flame. Charles pushed the pedal to the floor, the guttural rev of the car bounced off the trees and echoed through the night. Charles looked at the creature, the creature looked at him, but it was too late.

The car hit the creature at approximately 80 miles an hour, the two and a half-ton slab of metal batting the bluish corpse down the road, the body spinning like a log as it went, its arms limply flapping around and bouncing off the blacktop. Charles immediately slammed on the breaks, sliding several hundred feet as he stared in a skewed direction allowing him to keep both the tumbling body and Angelica in his periphery.

Leaving the engine running, Charles got out of the car, removed his sport jacket, and rolled up his sleeves. He opened the trunk and put on a black backpack with bandolier straps of shells over his shoulders. He grabbed a black double-barreled tactical shotgun and started walking toward the group of kids.

"Are you alright?" he asked Angelica. She just looked at him. With his free hand, he gently touched the side of her face and asked again, "Angelica, are you alright?"

Angelica fell against his chest, tears running down her face, "Yes. Yes. Thank you. Thank you."

"Who the fuck is this guy?" Brad asked, still looking at the road, down the trajectory the creature's body was thrown, eyes focused on the crumpled corpse illuminated by the Lincoln's headlights.

Angelica turned her face from buried in Charles's chest to the side and looked at Brad. "It's Charles, my Dad's husband, my stepfather."

Brad looked at Charles, having to cock his head up to make eye contact with him. "Well, Gay-Rambo, I have never been so happy to meet a friend's fucking parent in my whole fucking life."

Charles raised his eyebrows and smirked at the kid, but quickly switched to a look of confusion as he felt the hairs on his arms and neck stand on end.

The cutting metallic sound cut through the night air again, echoing through the forest as the headlights on the Lincoln went out.

"What was that?" Charles asked quietly, still hugging Angelica close.

"It's like an EMP or something, it turns out all the lights and electric shit," Brad answered. "It's been happening all night and it must be coming from, that, that thing." Brad pointed down the street to the silhouette of the crumpled corpse in the starlight.

Charles gently pushed Angelica away and dropped to his knees. He set down the shotgun and pulled several flashlights from the backpack. He handed the first one to Angelica, then one to Brad, and turned the third on and clicked it onto the side of the shotgun. Finally, he pulled a Beretta pistol from the bag, checked that it was loaded and that the safety was off, then handed it to Angelica.

The group pointed the three flashlights in the direction of the creature, looking on in silence. With the shotgun aimed at the corpse, Charles heard a crack like the breaking of bones. The heap of flesh rolled onto its hands and knees. It didn't have the shape of a body, more like a bag of skin with bones inside hanging over the extended limbs. With another crack, Charles could see that slowly but surely, the body was putting itself back together.

"I don't think this is over," Charles said to the kids, eyes still focused on the de-mangling in front of him.

"Shit," Carter and Tiffany said in unison.

"What are we going to do, Charles?" Angelica asked, her eyes wild with fear and exhaustion.

"We keep moving," he said to the group pointing in the opposite direction of the creatures cracking bones.

"Fuuuuuck," Brad moaned, "more running."

"Let's go," Charles ordered as the group started moving quickly back in the direction Charles initially came from.

"There's nothing out there. Where are we going?" Carter asked, attempting to sound reliable and in control, but his fear wobbled through.

"The only thing we are doing is creating distance, burning time. John and Harry should be here soon."

"Dad and Harry?" Angelica asked.

"Yes," Charles replied, "and when Harry gets here, he'll take over."

"So your car and your guns can't stop that freak, but this Harry can?" Brad questioned.

"Let's hope so," Charles answered.

As they moved, behind them they heard a chirping noise and then some kind of screech. Charles looked back and saw the reconstituted naked figure of the creature moving towards them. It moved quickly as Charles stepped toward it and yelled to the kids, "Run!"

They did as they were told. There was no talking, no arguing, and no complaining. Brad, Carter, and Tiffany knew that they wanted to live and that running was the best option for that. Angelica knew that Charles was a badass and that if Charles raised his voice even one decimal, then shit just got real.

At about fifteen yards Charles unloaded two shells at the creature. The 00 buck just slid and jellied over her skin like firing into gum, the skin rippling with the blast but snapping back to form. She kept moving, she was getting closer.

While Charles was an effective physical combat soldier, he was also an effective smart one. The first two of the twelve-round shotgun were loaded with buck, a good deterrent, the following four were not so friendly. He fired two rifled slugs, one at each of the she-beast's legs as she approached him. When the first struck it knocked it out from under her, but she was quick to recover. In Charles's good luck, before the leg could get good standing his second shot hit her other leg right in the knee snapping it back the other way. With her footing gone, the corpse fumbled forward and landed on her face right at Charle's feet. She tried to slash at his feet but he was already prepared. By the time her arm was halfway up, he had already placed both barrels at the back of her head. He pulled the triggers. Her head spread out like a squashed bug between the force of the blast and the asphalt beneath. He fired another round for good measure and started running to catch up with Angelica.

"Is it dead?" Angelica asked with a tremble.

"Fuck Me!" Brad yelled. "It's fucking still moving.

The legs of the corpse got to their knees and started pushing, trying to peel the creature's face from the ground. Her face released as she stood up and stumbled back a few steps. Her fanned out face and hideous rictus writhed and squirmed, slowing rearranging itself to its prior hideous visage.

"Keep moving," Charles shouted, but then stuck his arm out straight asking, "Do you hear that?"

They stopped and listened. Quiet at first, then, music bouncing off the trees and road, blues music?

A brown delivery truck came up the road toward them, music coming from the cab. The truck stopped next to them.

In the driver's seat was an old man in a newsboy, smoking a cigarette.

"This the place, Charles?" The man asked.

"Yes, Buster, you found us," Charles replied as the kids stared on in disbelief.

The old man slapped the side of the delivery truck and yelled, "Yo! Harry! We're here!"

The back door of the truck slid up as Harry stepped out followed by Thelonious. Harry was shirtless and shoeless, wearing only jeans, his black rune tattoos in stark contrast to his skin. Behind him, Thelonious in his robes looked down and prayed over his bowl of water. The pair walked up to Charles and the kids next to Buster in the cab.

Buster pointed at the blue corpse as it attempted to walk toward them in a roundabout confused circle, its smashed flat head's weight leading the way. "Apparently, it's that one," Buster said to Harry.

"Oh really?" Harry responded sarcastically.

The blue corpse of Biscuit started running at them and, in kind, Harry charged the creature.

Harry,
Down the Drain

Harry, Down the Drain

As Harry charged toward the blue corpse of the creature, that same metallic sound cut through the night like a buzzsaw, its dispersal of air blowing through Harry's close-cropped crew cut. The two supernatural powerhouses collided with a crack sending another blast of air at the onlookers, but for a strong start, it turned awry for Harry immediately. The creature's claws dug into his sides as she lifted him above her head and threw him into the Lincoln still parked in the middle of the highway.

Harry's body brutally smacked against the vehicle, denting in the side and tipping the car as Harry flipped over the top like a ragdoll. The creature looked at the car for a moment, her hideous smile dripping with saliva and blood, and then turned back to the group of kids and started quickly moving toward them.

"Of fuck," Brad said.

"Get behind the truck," Charles instructed, checking the shotgun.

From behind the truck came a cry of despondence. "My Car!!" The Professor stepped from the back of the brown delivery truck. "God damn it!"

"Dad!" Angelica yelled to him.

"Oh honey, are you okay?" he asked, running up to her as fast as his prematurely decrepit body would take him and putting his arms around her. He wiped her hair out of her face so as to get a good look at her.

"I've had better days," she told him.

"I bet you have," her father responded. "There's coffee and blankets in the back of the truck. You and your friends go rest up. Everything's okay now."

"Rest?" She looked at him in awe, "That thing is still coming at us!"

"What? What about Harry?"

"It killed him!" She cried.

"I sincerely doubt that," he said with a chuckle. The Professor yelled past the approaching creature to the mangled up car. "What the hell did you do to my car?"

From behind the smashed up car came Harry's disappointed voice, "Nope, I'm fine. Thanks for the concern!"

"Well it's still coming this way, so, hit it or something!" The Professor yelled.

"Hit or something, he says," Harry grumbled, brushing glass off his shoulders he walked toward the creature and yelled, "Hey! Naked Chick!"

The creature stopped and without moving her body twisted her waist pointing her shoulders, head, and maniacal grin back toward him.

"What the shit is this thing, Professor?" Harry shouted. "It's not infernal."

"No, it isn't," The Professor responded to him.

"You could have warned me!" Harry cried out, charging the creature, grabbing her around the waist and whipping her back, tossing her toward the car. Harry's throw didn't send her as far and she landed on her feet like a cat in front of the vehicle. "Great," Harry mumbled to himself through panting.

"He's not going to be able to stop it," Charles said to The Professor grabbing his hand. "We all have to get out of here immediately."

The Professor looked at Charles for a moment, and then at the group of kids stumbling through his words. "I… I… don't… we can't just leave Harry?"

Next to the two Tiffany is stumbling backward, eyes locked on the rumble down the road talking to herself, "Why won't it leave us alone? Why? Why won't it leave us alone?"

Charles and The Professor made eye contact.

"It's not a bad question," The Professor says. "Watch the kids." Charles just looks at him a bit dumbfounded, mouth open and arms out as The Professor walks away from them and toward Thelonious.

"Can you tell me what it wants?" he asked Thelonious straight up.

Staring at the bowl, Thelonious thought for a moment and without looking up said, "I would have to drop the protection spell over Harry."

"How long would it take him to find us?" The Professor asked.

"I just don't know, Professor," Thelonious responded, "we have never tried before."

The Professor looked Thelonious in the eyes and said, "Do it?"

"But, what of Harry," Thelonious responded with incertitude in his voice.

From twenty yards away they heard Harry's labored yell,

"Just do it Man! This chick is whooping my ass!"

Thelonious took his hand from the side of the bowl, put it directly in the water, and looked directly at the creature. In the far distance, there was a lightning-less crash of thunder that echoed through the forest.

He returned his hand to the side of the bowl and yelled out, "She is confused, she's not supposed to be here. Part of her is of here and part of her is not."

"What the hell is that supposed to mean? How is that supposed to help me stop it?" The Professor questioned. "Find out how to stop the thing!"

Again, Thelonious removed his hand from the side of the bowl and placed it in the water. Again there was a shudder of thunder that barreled through the trees, this time closer and even louder than before. The monk's stern eyes focused on the creature in the battle before them, his mind's eye, his astral self flopped between Harry and the creature, filling his head with flashes, flashes that must be deciphered.

Flash, a young child, flash a black lake, flash a lake of fire, flash a motherly woman, the kids, a glowing gem, a wooden staff. With each flash he tries to get closer, he tries to go deeper. He reaches out trying to grasp onto something desperately but it is all just out of reach. He snapped out one more time turning and stretching reaching out with fingertips trying to grasp and he went. It's not a full grip, more of a touch really, just the brushing of his fingertips against something solid in the astral plane. He returned his hand to the side of the bowl and said, "I can make her forget"

The Professor looked at him after the statement, his face a mix-mash of expressing to Thelonious, "Just fucking do it!" and "Why the hell are you even taking the time to tell me this?".

For the final time, Thelonious removed his hand from the side of the bowl and placed it in the water. For the final time, his astral self snapped from his body, but this time made a direct trajectory towards the creature. Arms out he grasped at everything in her he could. Through the light and the shadow that was her astral self, he snatched what he could. Whisps and plumes and beams and rays, he pulled and grabbed at them like wires and tubes in an ethereal machine.

The creature stopped. Her smile remained, but her brow dropped ever so slightly. Then, with no indication, she looked up at the stars, looked back at the monk with somehow an even bigger smile, and slowly walked into the forest. All of them watched in silent awe as what was once Biscuit disappeared into the brush.

The silence was broken by the same crack of thunder with no lightning through the night air. This time the sound was practically on top of them. The Professor quickly looked at Thelonious. The monk nodded his head down and started praying over the bowl of water again.

"In the truck," The Professor demanded as Charles herded the kids in. Thelonious waited for Harry as he backstepped to the truck, keeping his eyes on the creature as it walked into the wilderness as though nothing had happened.

"You're not coming?" Harry asked The Professor.

"John," Charles said walking toward him.

"You know I have to do this and your job is to watch Angelica just in case the 'this I have to do' doesn't work."

Charles looked at him and then got in the truck with Angelica.

Angelica popped her head out of the back of the truck with a blanket over her shoulders and a steaming paper cup of coffee. "Dad, you're not coming?"

"No, I'll catch a different ride," The Professor answered. "I need to finish up here, Honey. I'll meet you back at the house." He slapped the side of the truck and Buster got the truck moving.

Charles, Thelonious, and Harry hopped in the slowly departing truck and Charles gently forced Angelica away from the door. Harry leaned his head back out, looking to The Professor, "Thank you, Professor. I'll keep a light on for ya."

"Don't worry about it," The Professor assured him, waving him off dispassionately as the truck gained speed and whisked away around the corner.

The Professor reached into his jacket's breast pocket and pulled out two cigars. Again, he heard the crack of thunder with no lightning, and from the darkness of the shadows around him a man in a black suit stepped from the shadow.

"Good evening, Jonathan," the man said. His skin was light, almost grey, with a finely trimmed beard and mustache.

"Oh, what are you doing here, Incubus?" The Professor feigned surprise. He offered the demon one of the cigars.

"Very funny, John," Incubus replied, reaching up his grey hand with pointed black, perfectly manicured nails and taking the offered cigar.

Both the men put the cigars in their mouths as Incubus passed his hand over each one and the tips started to smoke.

"It must be nice to not have to carry so much shit around in your pockets" The Professor stated with a nod at the demon's hands.

"You know I like you, Jonathan. The enemy of my enemy and all that," Incubus said, drawing heavily on the cigar.

The Professor dropped the niceties, "What do you want?"

"How many times must we have this conversation? You know what I want. I want Harry back." Incubus said with an almost undetectable amount of joy in his voice.

"Well, he isn't here," The Professor said through an exhale of thick, bitter smoke.

"He was here. I felt him," Incubus put a hand on his chest and closed his eyes. He inhaled deeply through his nose. "And I can smell the stench of Chaos from the other world, so I can pretty much assume I know what he was doing here."

"Not that I know where he is, but what do you assume he was doing here?"

"Bailing you out of a mess," Incubus said flatly, staring at The Professor in the eyes. "You or maybe your transgressive lover, that Charles. Oh, I do like him, such an interesting combination of nobility and sin." Incubus paused, still looking directly into The Professor's eyes with his orange irises. "Or maybe helping a daughter, John?" He asked.

"You leave her out of this. She has nothing to do with anything," The Professor stated defensively, not able to shake the demon's gaze.

"Oh don't worry, John," Incubus crooned, "She's the only truly good one in the lot of you. I don't think I could touch her if I tried thanks to our other little friend," the demon's voice started as a pleasant coo but slowly turned into an animalistic growl as he said, "but I am not the type of man

85

that rewards good deeds or the type of man that forgets transgressions... and I want Harry."

The professor wanted to look away, but couldn't break the leer of Incubus.

"I will get him eventually. We both know that." The demon continued, "and I will be seeing you and your little hubby again too." He blinked and the involuntary staring contest was broken. "Have a good night, John." Incubus walked away down the street in the direction of the truck, disappearing into the shadows with another lightning-less clap of thunder.

Gripping the cigar with his teeth, The Professor reached in his pocket and pulled out his phone. He dialed and waited for the ring. There was a click as the phone was answered, but no salutation hello, only silence.

"I'm ready to be picked up," he sighed into the phone.

"Yes, sir," from the other end, "Fifteen minutes out."

"Okay," and The Professor hung up. He dialed again.

"Fort Hoag Reception, How can I help you?" from the other end.

"I need to speak with Brigadier General Higuchi," The Professor told the receptionist.

"I'm sorry sir, the Brigadier General is not available"

"Well, find him, wherever he is, and tell him John Wateley Called. Sierra, Oscar, Sierra, Victor," The Professor mumbled and hung up the phone. He returned the phone to his pocket, sat down on the pavement finishing his cigar, and waited for his ride.

ART

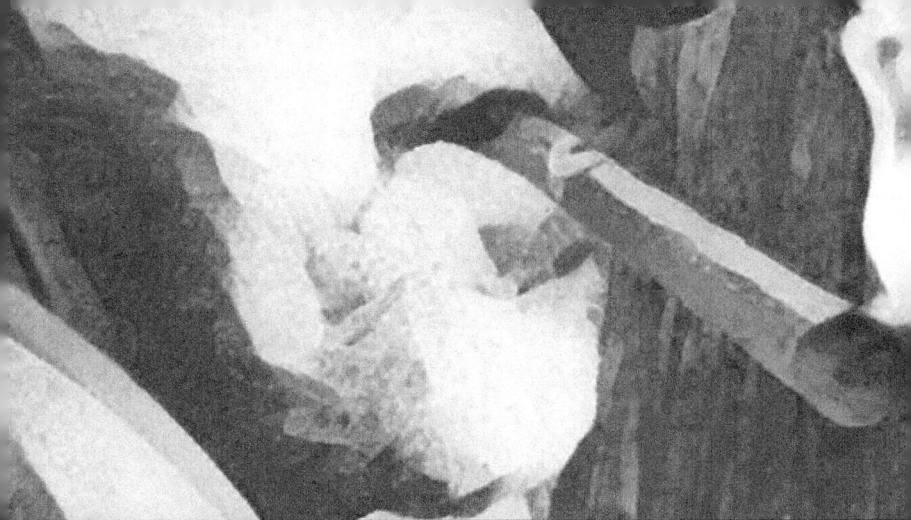

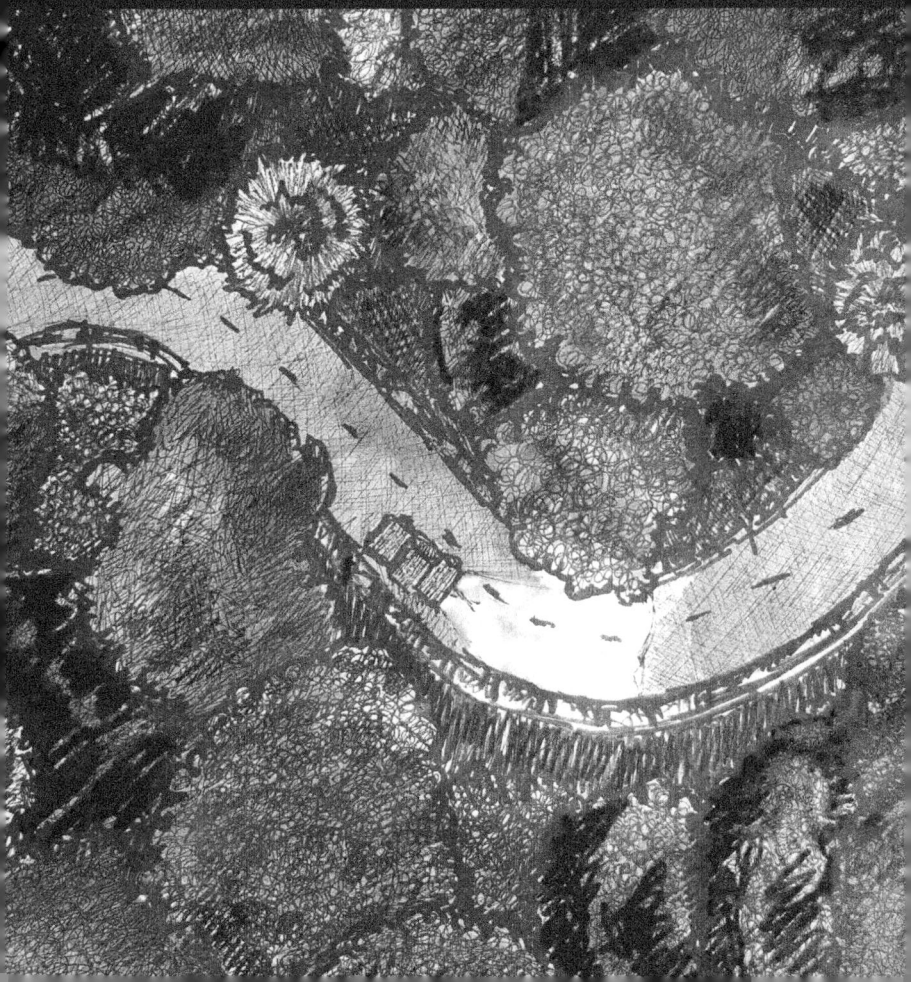

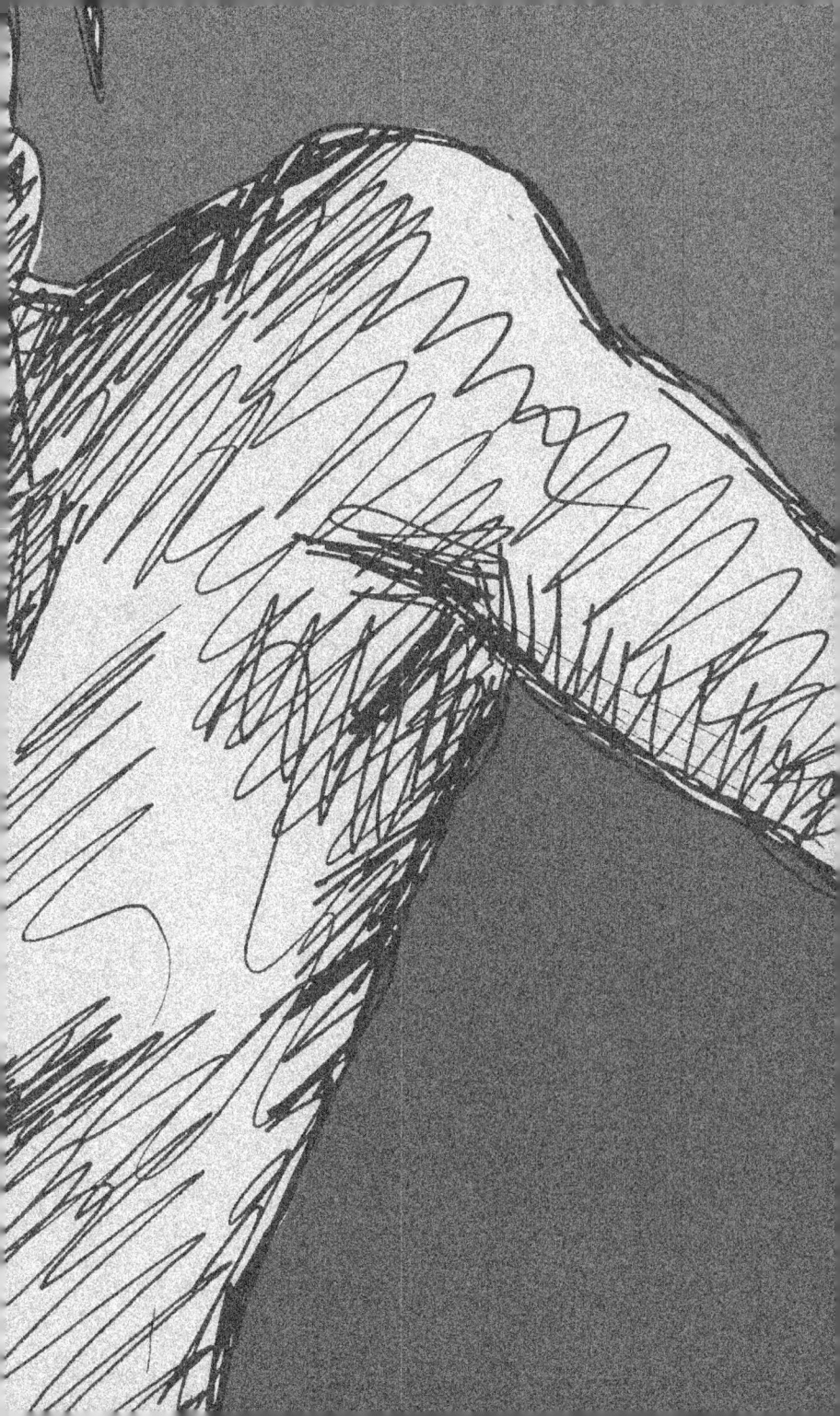

RIGHT THERE
BY YOUR SIDE

DOWN THE DRAIN

Coming Up:

The Society

After taking what he felt might have been a contender for one of the longest pisses of his life, Johnny washed his face in the sink. The cold water did a pretty good job of settling his nerves, and his settled nerves did a pretty good job of making him feel like a fool.

He sighed into his reflection and gave himself a mocking smirk. He reached in his pocket and pulled out his cell phone, spying a stall, he sat down on the closed toilet seat and started checking his messages.

He texted Ivan, "This place suuuuuux!" He hit send, leaned his head back, and gave another good quality exhale through his comforting smirk. Then, the chirp followed by the vibratory trill of his phone receiving a reply. The beep and buzz echoed through the tile bathroom like a bell in a cavernous church, the sound scaring him to the point his heart skipped a beat. He frantically rubbed his thumb up the side of the phone desperately trying to get to the volume, but not wanting to go too far. He found it and pressed it, holding it down until it quietly vibrated and then even the vibrating was stopped. The room was again silent. Then, he heard the creak of the restroom door. He quickly pulled his feet up onto the toilet and with his free hand, reached out and grabbed the stall door and slowly pulled it toward him, not wanting to lock it and make a sound. He teetered there, balanced on the top of the toilet, feet on the lid, cell phone gripped in one hand and the other holding the stall door shut.

Outside the stall, he could hear a woman breathing, almost like she was gasping for air through a veil of water, the labored, gargled breathing being drawn closer on the clop of wooden heels slowly clicking across the tile floor. Looking down, below his arm holding the door shut he could see his shoes barely perched on the porcelain lid, he could see his phone in his other dangling hand, with the notification from Ivan, "How so?". He could see the shadow the breathing woman cast, closer and closer under the stall door until with another set of wooden clops she stopped. He could see the breathing woman's wood-heeled, puritan shoes. They were polished black to the point where he could make out his reflection, not the details, just the clouded shape of his face. A shape that in detail he would hardly recognize through its frozen distorted look of fear.

The breathing stopped.

A pale hand with long, well-manicured nails slowly crept around the bottom of the bathroom stall door, Johnny's eyes sprung even wider, staring at the hand's deliberate movement in horror. The hand jostled the door, but Johnny pushed his weight into it, his shoes silently slipping across the toilet seat.

The hand stopped moving. Above the shoes, the shadow grew darker and tighter and Johnny knew that it was her body, moving her head to the floor, coming closer, so that she could see beneath.

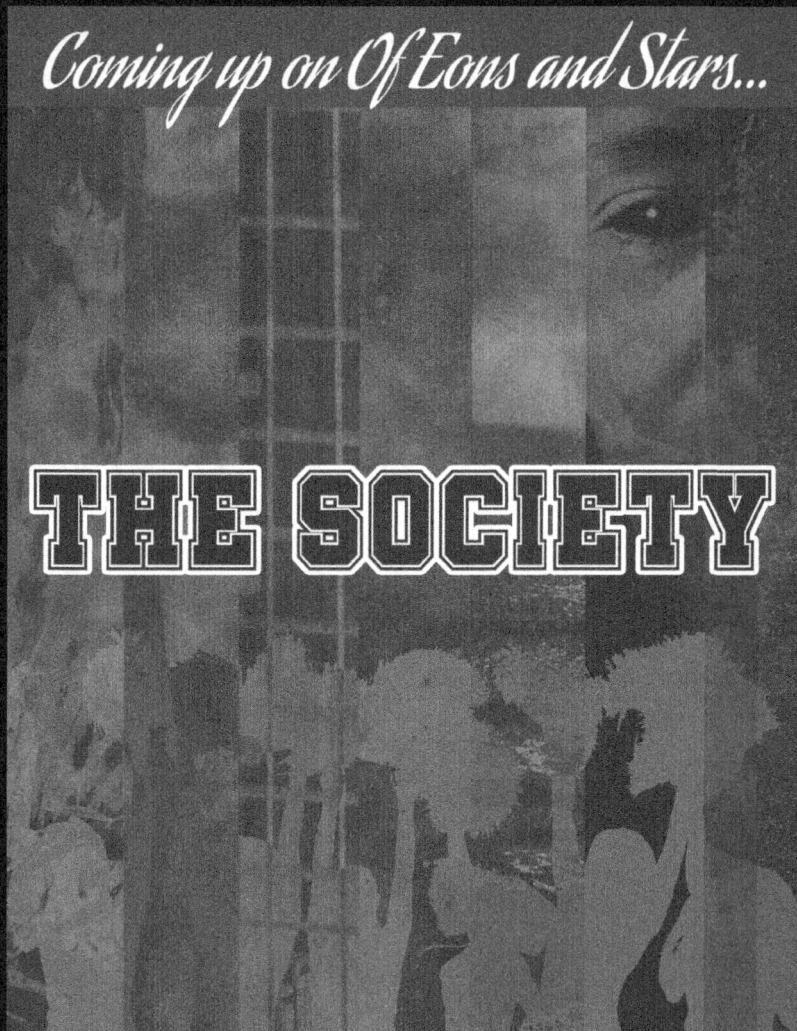

Coming up on *Of Eons and Stars...*

THE SOCIETY

Coming up on *Of Eons and Stars...*

THE COSMIC SEED

Made in the USA
Middletown, DE
01 April 2021